KEEPING
CHRISTMAS

KEEPING CHRISTMAS

STORIES OF THE JOYOUS SEASON

selected by
PHYLLIS R. FENNER

Illustrated by Honi Werner

William Morrow and Company   New York 1979

Copyright © 1979 by Phyllis R. Fenner

Grateful acknowledgment is made for permission to quote from the following:

"The Riders of St. Nicholas" by Jack Schaefer. Copyright © 1961 by Jack Schaefer. Reprinted by permission of Harold Matson Company, Inc.

"The Road to St. Vivien" from MORE COMBAT STORIES OF WORLD WAR II AND KOREA by William Chamberlain (John Day). Copyright 1954, © 1958, 1959, 1960, 1961, 1962 by The Curtis Publishing Company. Copyright © 1964 by William Chamberlain. Reprinted by permission of Harper & Row, Publishers, Inc.

"Barren Christmas" by Olaf Ruhen. Copyright 1955 by The Curtis Publishing Company. Reprinted by permission of *The Saturday Evening Post*.

"Christmas Day in the Morning" by Pearl S. Buck. Copyright 1955 by Pearl S. Buck. Reprinted by permission of Harold Ober Associates, Incorporated.

"The Christmas Present" by Gordon R. Dickson. Reprinted by permission of the author.

"Francie Nolan's Christmas Tree" by Betty Smith. Copyright 1943, 1947 by Betty Smith. From pp. 168-177 in A TREE GROWS IN BROOKLYN. Reprinted by permission of Harper & Row, Publishers, Inc.

"The Christmas Doll" by B. J. Chute. Reprinted by permission of the author.

"Greetings from A. Bledsoe Smith" by Irene Kampen. Copyright © 1960 by Irene Kampen. Reprinted by permission of International Creative Management.

"The Last Delivery Before Christmas" by Ernest Buckler. Reprinted by permission of The Canadian Publishers, McClelland and Stewart Limited, Toronto.

"The Theft of the Royal Ruby" by Agatha Christie. Copyright © 1960 by Agatha Christie Ltd. Reprinted by permission of Dodd, Mead & Company, Inc. from DOUBLE SIN AND OTHER STORIES.

Printed in the United States of America.   1 2 3 4 5 6 7 8 9 10

Library of Congress Cataloging in Publication Data

Main entry under title:
Keeping Christmas
Contents: Schaefer, J. The riders of Saint Nicholas.—Chamberlain, W. The road to St. Vivien.—Ruhen, O. Barren Christmas. [etc.]
1. Christmas stories. [1. Christmas stories]
I. Fenner, Phyllis Reid, 1899-   II. Werner, Honi.
PZ5.K37   [Fic]   79-15590
ISBN 0-688-22206-4   ISBN 0-688-32206-9 lib. bdg.

Merry Christmas
to
Helen P. Pearson
with a gift of friendship

CONTENTS

"Merry merry merry Christmas Bells
Oh sweetly sweetly chime"

Plum pudding, roast goose, wassail bowl, boar's head, the lighting of candles, holly wreaths, store windows filled with toys for the children to gaze at with hope, Santa Clauses ringing their bells on street corners, Christmas carols in the air, yearly messages from faraway friends—all announce Christmas.

There are some to whom the holiday means nothing, some who like it superficially, and some who love it deeply. These last people make loving preparations for The Day with an uplift of spirit that no other time brings. The very "Merry Christmas" that they call out to others is a sign of their joyous state of mind. In fact, Christmas *is* a state of mind as much as a festival.

To all who love the joyous season, I say, "Merry Christmas!"

P.F.

THE RIDERS
OF SAINT NICHOLAS

Jack Schaefer

The day dawned still and clear, with the winter-night chill of the high country lingering in the air. Stringy clouds clung to the tops of the mountains to the west, but that was nothing unusual in late December. The sun below the horizon to the east sent edgings of color along the high-hanging clouds, and the first pink flush of a fine morning touched the roof of the cookhouse in which the men of the Slash Y were finishing a particularly hearty breakfast.

Range manager Cal Brennan set down his coffee cup and pulled a paper bag from a jacket pocket and shook it gently. A soft rattling sound came from it. "I ain't takin' the trouble," he said, "of decidin' who's goin' an' who's stayin'. I'm makin' it an even chance for everybody, in-cludin' Cookie here an' myself too. There's thirteen of us, an' there's thirteen beans in here. Ten white an' three brown. White ones go. Brown ones stay."

He held the bag up in his left hand above eye level and reached into it with his right hand. The hand emerged holding a white bean between thumb and forefinger. "Well, well," he said. "Bein' nice about this's paid off nice too." He passed the bag to foreman Hat Henderson.

Hat held it up, reached into it. A white bean. "Reckon I live right," he said, and passed the bag to Monte Walsh.

Monte held it up. "Gambling's a sin," he said. "That's what my mother used to say. Must be true 'cause I never have any luck at it." He reached in. A brown bean. "See what I mean?" he said. "And I got new boots too."

"No bellyaching," said Powder Kent, taking the bag. A white bean. "Don't fret, Monte. Miss Annie won't even miss you. Not with me there."

The bag passed on around the long table. White beans. Sunfish Perkins held it up. A brown bean. "Aw, hell," he said. "I ain't much on dancing and such anyways."

The bag passed on. Chet Rollins held it up. Two beans

14

left in it—a white and a brown. Chet's glance flicked across the table at Monte—slumped on the bench staring down in disgust at the bean in his hand—and flicked back to the bag. He reached in. It could have been a white bean emerging between his thumb and forefinger, but before anyone was quite certain it slipped from his fingers back into the bag. "Damn," murmured Chet cheerfully, and reached in again. A brown bean. He tossed the bag to Skimpy Eagens, the cook. "It's all yours," he said.

The sun was an hour up, warming the air, driving the night chill back into the mountains. Monte Walsh and Chet Rollins and Sunfish Perkins sat on a top corral rail, watching the ten white-bean winners saddle up. The ten had a forty-five-mile ride ahead of them, but what was a mere forty-five miles to the prospect of Christmas Eve festivities at the headquarters of the Triple Seven, for which folks were gathering from an even wider radius?

"You know," said Monte, morose, "I been thinking. That bag game wasn't exactly fair. First pickers had best chances, what with more white beans still in there. I'll bet Cal had that figured."

"Sure," said Chet. "But you can't squawk much. You were one of the first."

Monte gnawed on a knuckle. "That just goes to show," he said. "Luck and me ain't even acquainted. Someday I'm going to—" He stopped. Skimpy Eagens had left his horse and was calling to him.

"Come along, Monte," said Skimpy. "Something to show you." He led the way toward the cookhouse.

Inside, on the plank shelf near the big wood stove, limp, well-washed flour sacks were tucked down over two humped objects. Skimpy removed one with a flourish, disclosing the plump carcass of a wild turkey in a battered roasting pan.

15

"Cal brought that in two days ago," he said. "It's stuffed. All you got to do is get a good fire going and put it in. About two hours. A little basting'd help."

"Basting?" said Monte, somewhat brightened.

"Just scoop up hot juice and dribble it over," said Skimpy. He lifted the second covering, disclosing a squat, dark ball of pudding in another pan. "Course those plums ain't fresh, only canned. But there's a snitch of brandy in it. Just warm it up some."

"What do you know," said Monte, brightening more.

"Not till tomorrow," said Skimpy. "That's what they're for. And maybe I'll show you something else. Cal figured to let you just find it when you started rooting for food, but maybe he's hoping you'd just miss it." Skimpy pulled open a bulging potato bag under the shelf and took out an un-opened bottle of whisky.

"That," said Monte, beaming, "is the best yet. I'll just take charge of that right now."

"You can read, can't you?" said Skimpy, holding the bottle up. A small piece of paper was flattened around it with a tag end of string. On the paper was written in Cal Brennan's crabbed scrawl, "Not to be opened till Christmas."

"All right," said Monte. "But put that thing back quick."

"Too late," said Sunfish Perkins from the doorway. "I got a good look."

The sun was an hour and a half up, warming the air, reaching for the rim of frost left by the night chill around the inside of the corral water trough. Monte Walsh and Chet Rollins and Sunfish Perkins sat on the same top rail, watching the dust of the ten white-bean winners fade off northward.

"Hope that horse of Powder's stumbles and breaks a leg," said Monte. "The leg being Powder's."

Silence along the rail.

"Know what I'm going to do?" said Monte. "Soon as it warms up more, I'm going over to the house and bring that leather chair of Cal's out on the porch and sit in the sun. I'm going to catch up some on the sitting I ain't done in a long time. I'm going to sit there thinking of how Hat's been working us these last weeks. I'm going to sit there thinking up ways of talking you two into bringing me food so I don't even have to move none. Then I'm going to sit there some more, trying to make up my mind should I slip into town tonight or just take over that bed of Cal's and catch up on all that sleep I missed last month riding line extra for Dobe 'cause of that bad ankle of his."

Silence along the rail.

"Yep," said Monte. "That's it. And tomorrow if I feel up to it, maybe I'll show you two how easy I can beat you at horseshoes. That seems kind of strenuous right about now, but maybe I'll do it just to work up the right kind of appetite for that turkey and pudding and the other fixings you two'll fix."

"Sounds terrible exciting," said Sunfish. "Then what'll you do?"

"Why, shucks," said Monte. "Then I'll just sit some more and see how much mileage I can get out of my third of that bottle."

Silence along the rail.

"Well, now," said Chet, staring down solemnly at his hands on his knees. "Hat mentioned something about rehanging those crooked barn doors. Also something about working over the harness gear."

Monte shifted sideways some to stare at Chet.

17

Jack Schaefer

"And also again and likewise," said Chet, "something about putting a new gate on that other corral."

Monte stared at Chet, horrified. "You mean," he said, "you're thinking of us killing ourselves working while the rest of 'em are off having fun?"

"Why, no," said Chet. "Did I say I was? But Hat mentioned those things, so I figured I ought at least do the same."

"Right," said Monte. "You've mentioned 'em. Now what's it really you're thinking of doing?"

"Sitting on that porch in the sun," said Chet. "Maybe playing a little euchre with you two so's to settle who cooks when. But mostly just sitting."

"Me too," said Sunfish Perkins.

The sun was well past noon, the sunlight warm and reassuring. Monte Walsh sat on the ranch-house porch, limp and lazy, in the mouse-chewed remnants of a once-imposing leather-covered armchair. A few feet away Chet Rollins leaned back, equally limp and lazy, in a rocker padded with the remains of old saddle blankets. Both chairs were placed at precise angles for maximum sunlight benefit. A few more feet away Sunfish Perkins sat cross-legged on the porch floor, leaning forward to play solitaire with an old, worn deck of cards.

"My, oh, my," murmured Monte. "It tires me just to hear him. Where's he get the energy to slap those cards so loud? How's he doing it with all that fat around his middle?"

"No fat," said Sunfish without looking up. "Muscle."

"Oh, my, yes," murmured Monte. "The kind of muscle they pack into lard pails."

Silence on the porch—a companionable silence broken only by the soft plop of old cards on old cards.

Over in the first corral a horse whinnied. On the porch three heads lifted some and looked into the distances of the big land. A darkish speck moved against the seemingly endless reaches of plain to the southeast.

"He got a late start," said Monte. "That is, if he's aiming at the doings up north."

"What's he doing heading over here then?" said Chet.

Silence on the porch. Sunfish gathered up the cards and leaned back against the porch post. The speck became larger and was a man on a horse.

"Simple," said Monte. "The horse's lame."

"G'wan," said Sunfish. "You can't tell this far."

"Want to bet?" said Monte. "It's favoring the off fore-foot."

Silence on the porch. The man and the horse came closer, and they were Sonny Jacobs of the Diamond Six and a smallish neat sorrel definitely favoring its off fore-foot. They stopped by the porch, and Sonny surveyed its occupants. A wide smile creased his broad young face. "I never thought to see the day," he said. "Damned if you don't look like three old ladies sitting around at a sewing circle."

"That's better'n you look," said Monte. "Which is plain foolish, expecting to get anywheres on one of those bat-brained horses you raise down your way. What'd it do, step in a badger hole?"

"Hell, no," said Sonny. "Shied at a rabbit and into some damned cactus. I worked on that pastern maybe half a hour, but must be some spines still in it. You got anything particular to say about which one of yours I take?"

"Shucks, no," said Monte. "Any one you want in the corral there, long as it's the gray."

Three heads turned slightly to watch Sonny ride to the corral, dismount, open the gate, lead the sorrel in. His saddle rose into view from inside, heaved up to rest on a top rail. Dust rose over the corral, and a rope flashed through it. The saddle disappeared down inside, and Sonny came out leading a biggish, mean-looking gray. He swung up and rocked in the saddle as the horse plunged forward, bucking. Four lively minutes later he sat serenely in saddle by the porch as the horse stood quivering under him. "You sure can pick 'em, Monte boy," he said. "He'll be right interesting."

"And go the distance," said Monte. "You sure you ain't afraid of him?"

"Plumb scared to death," said Sonny. He reared the gray spinning on hind legs and started away fast and swung back in a short circle. "Almost forgot to tell you. I came up your east range. Following the drift fence. There's a stretch of it down." He swung again and was gone.

Silence on the porch. Three men sat still, very still, looking at one another and away. "Damn," said Sunfish.

"No, sir," said Monte. "I ain't going to move. Let it stay down awhile. When the others get back'll be time enough."

Chet sighed. "Yes-s-s-s," he said. "Yes, I guess maybe it will."

The sun was well into the afternoon, the sunlight full on the porch. Monte Walsh reclined in the remnants of an armchair, eyes closed. Chet Rollins reclined in the old rocker, head dropped sideways, breath coming in sighs not quite strong enough to be called snores. Sunfish Perkins lay full length on a doubled-over old quilt, definitely snoring in long, slow rhythm.

Monte opened his eyes, blinking into the sunlight. "Funny," he murmured. "Sun's right up there right on the job, but I feel kind of chilly around the edges." He closed his eyes again.

Slowly, then with increasing swiftness, the sunlight faded. Over by the other buildings a loose piece of roofing tin rattled. A gust of wind, whirling, picking up dust, swept past the porch. Monte opened his eyes and raised his head some. He sat up straighter. His eyes focused into distance to the west. "Chet," he said, voice low and urgent. "Take a look."

Chet snapped out of sleep and straightened, looking. Off to the west the mountains were gone, erased in a great drab grayness that filled the horizon and obscured the sun. Another gust swept past, and in the following stillness, suddenly heavy and ominous, Sunfish Perkins grunted and pushed up from the porch floor and stood looking too.

"Coming this way," said Sunfish, shivering. "And colder by the minute. Must be snow in it."

"That ain't good," said Monte. "It ain't good at all."

"Sure not," said Chet. "If this turns into something and any cows get through that fence, they'll drift with it clean over into Texas."

"Aw, hell," said Sunfish. "And I was dreaming so nice."

"Finish it later," said Chet. "What've we got in the corral?"

"Two apiece," said Monte. "That is, we did have before Sonny stole one. Come along."

Ten minutes later the three of them, in heavy jackets, gloved, hats pulled well down, led three horses, saddled, out of the near corral. Over the saddle horn of Monte's rat-tailed roan hung a coil of light baling wire. The wind came in long sweeps now, and the sky steadily darkened.

"Sunfish," said Chet. "This gets bad like it looks it could, we'll be needing plenty of relays the next day or two. You swing out and bring in some more of the saddle stock. Six or eight, anyway. Then you can get a fire going in the house where likely we'll hole up and get something hot cooking. Monte and me, we'll get that fence."

"Got you," said Sunfish. He swung up and left at a lope around the corner of the corral.

"Shucks," said Monte. "Looks like his bean wasn't as brown as mine. Yours too. Bring in a few horses. Cook a meal. And we got five, six miles just to get there. Then there's ten miles of fence."

"Sonny rode it," said Chet. "Mentioned one stretch down. One. Could be in the first mile." He swung up and started off.

"With my luck," said Monte, mounting, "it'll be the last mile."

Under the darkening sky, wind moved over the big land, whipping the short winter-cured grasses. The first flurries of snow skittered with it, big-flaked, hardening as the temperature dropped. Like a long, blurred pencil mark across the bigness, the drift fence came out of distance and went into distance, not so much a discernible fence as a line of tumbleweed banked against the poles and wires. Where some violent freak of wind, likely an oversize dust devil, had smashed sometime recently against massed tumbleweed and used it as a battering ram to rip the wires loose from the posts, a rat-tailed roan and a chunky bay stood, heads drooping, rumps hunched into the wind. Not far away two men worked rapidly, alternating at posts, wire cutters in hand, tugging to lift the sagging barbed-wire with which to lash each strand and snipping short lengths of bailing wire with which to lash each strand back into place on the posts.

The wind rose, and the snow increased, small-flaked now and hard and stinging, and two tough little cow ponies waited, and two men, fingers numbing, worked steadily on down the line. And across the darkening miles, back by the ranch buildings, another man, big barrel body swinging in saddle, raced on a sweat-streaked mottled roan to pocket a batch of skittery horses in an angle of fence, push them through a gate into the big holding corral, follow them in and close the gate, open another at the other end and work them on into the smaller, regular horse corral.

Swirling snow, wind-driven, filled the darkness of early night, making a grayness in which vision died at fifteen feet. A rat-tailed roan and a chunky bay, sleet-crusted, pushed through the grayness at a steady jog. The men in the saddles were hunched low, jacket collars up, hats pulled down with short lengths of baling wire over the crowns and ends twisted together under their chins, holding the brims down over their ears.

The roan raised its head and looked to the right, snorting snow out of its nostrils and whinnying.

"Look there," said Monte Walsh, drawing rein. "What now?"

"What say?" shouted Chet Rollins, stopping beside him.

Off to the right, lost in the swirling grayness, a horse whinnied. They swerved right and advanced slowly, peering ahead. They stopped. Directly in front of them stood a small, scrawny horse, showing pinto through the patches of snow gathering on it.

"Ain't that one of Gonzales's?" said Monte.

"And saddled," said Chet. "What's holding him?"

The horse sidled around to face more toward them and

raised its head. One rein hung limp. The other drew taut, fastened to some object on the ground rapidly becoming indistinguishable under a mantle of snow.

In one swift motion Monte was down and striding forward. In one swift matching motion Chet had swung down in the saddle and scooped up the reins of Monte's horse. He watched as Monte bent low, following the taut rein of the other horse down, fumbling to untie it from around a man's wrist. He watched as Monte brushed snow aside and heaved, rolling the object over so that the whiteness of a face under an old cap looked up into the swirling snow.

"José?" said Chet.

"Who else?" said Monte, dropping to his knees and bending lower.

"Alive?" said Chet.

"Yeah," said Monte. "And drunk. Smells like a damned saloon."

"Sober enough to hang onto the horse," said Chet. "Maybe the cold caught him too. That ain't much of a coat he's got."

"Yeah," said Monte. "Be stiffer'n a poker in another hour like this." Moving swiftly, Monte stepped to the roan and, with fumbling gloved fingers, began to unloosen the cinch. "What d'you figure he's been doing out here?"

"Been into town," said Chet. "Stayed too long. Too many primos and too much vino. Likely he was getting some things for the kids. Tomorrow's Christmas, or have you forgot?"

"I been trying to forget," said Monte, pulling the saddle blanket from under his saddle. He spread the blanket on the snow-covered ground and rolled the limp body of José Gonzales onto it. "Funny, ain't it," he said, "the fool

24

things people'll do for kids." He wrapped the blanket around tight. "That'll help some around the middle anyways," he said, and picked up the wrapped body and laid it, belly down, over the saddle on the pinto. A half-full burlap hanging from the saddle horn was in the way. He unlooped it and handed it to Chet.

The central room of the old adobe ranch house was warm and cheerful in the light of two kerosene lamps and a fire in the huge stone fireplace. Three straw mattresses and a pile of blankets from the bunkhouse were ranged on the floor along the wall. A fair-sized iron kettle and a wide flat pan and a big coffeepot sat on the raised hearth. One whole front corner of the room was filled with fragrant piñon firewood.

Monte Walsh sat in the mouse-chewed remnants of armchair on one side of the fireplace, working on his seventh biscuit, his third cup of coffee, his second bowl of the Sunfish specialty—stewed beef swimming in a sauce of mashed beans. Sunfish Perkins himself sat in the old rocker on the other side of the fireplace, watching with considerable interest the activity near the closed front door. There, well away from the fire, the meager body of José Gonzales, stripped naked, lay on the floor. His worn clothing, patched long underwear and ragged jeans and shirt and thin coat, was draped over a ladder-back chair before the fire. His half-full burlap bag sagged against the front wall by the door. Beside him knelt Chet Rollins, rubbing his bare arms and legs with melting snow from a nearby pail.

"Gosh," said Sunfish. "There ain't much of him, is there?"

"Not exactly in your overweight class," said Monte. "But

25

there's enough of him to have more'n any of us's got—a wife and two kids."

"And a sister," said Sunfish. "Dobe'd never let you forget that."

José moaned and kicked feebly with one foot. "Go ahead, kick," said Chet. "I know it hurts like hell thawing out."

"And he eats prodigious," said Monte. "Looks like we got another boarder till this thing lets up."

"I ain't hauling in no other mattress," said Sunfish. "He can have yours. We'll just take you up on that talk about Cal's bed. You'll freeze your gizzard in that little room with no fire, but you'll freeze fancy."

José's head raised a bit and thumped back on the floor, and he began to thrash about in aimless motion. "Well, well," said Chet. "So you're wiggling all of them now." He picked up a piece of toweling and began rubbing with it.

"Shucks, Chet," said Monte, ambling over. "You got to eat too. I'll wrassle with him some."

Sunfish heaved to his feet and began to serve up stew and biscuits and coffee. "What's he got in that bag?" he said.

"A little food," said Chet, settling into the armchair to start on his first bowl of the Sunfish special. "A few things for the kids."

"It ain't much," said Monte suddenly, sharply, looking up from his rubbing. The other two stared at him. "Aw, shucks," he said, returning to work. "Tomorrow's Christmas, ain't it?"

Silence in the big old room.

"It's sure doing things outside," said Sunfish. "Must of been four inches already when you came in. Maybe it'll be like that one two years ago."

"Colder," said Chet. "That ought to mean less snow."

José opened his eyes and stared unaware at the ceiling. He turned away on his side, muttering bitterly in Spanish.

"No cussing," said Monte. "That ain't polite. Reckon you're about ready to try navigating some." He slipped an arm under the thin shoulders and rose, bringing José up with him. José wobbled on bare feet and reached out instinctively to brace himself against the front wall.

"Exercise," said Monte. "That's what you need. Walking'll do it." He began propelling him across the floor, back and forth.

"Easy," said Chet around a mouthful of stew. "Slow down. He ain't made of cast iron like you."

Moving his feet mechanically, José looked up vacantly at Monte.

"Aw, come on," said Monte cheerfully. "You're doing fine. Stepping out like a trooper." He propelled José over by the ladder-back chair and released the arm holding him, ready to grab again.

José stood steady enough, staring down at the clothes on the chair as if unaware of what they were.

"Quit it now," said Monte sternly. "Don't you go being stupid on me. It's plumb indecent the way you're parading around here. Put those things on."

Mechanically, moving out of old habit, José began dressing.

"Well, lookathere," said Sunfish. "Monte, you get too old to straddle a hoss, you can hire out as nursemaid."

José had on the patched underwear, the ragged pants and shirt. He picked up one of the boots and sat down on the chair as if to put it on and simply sat there, holding the boot, staring into the fire.

"Still being stupid, eh?" said Monte. "I ought to bat you one. Want to roast yourself?" He took hold of the chair

27

and pulled it and José in it back to a safe distance, and José simply sat there, holding the boot, staring into the fire.

"All I got to say," said Sunfish, "is he's going to be mighty exciting company if he stays that way."

"He'll snap out of it," said Chet. "Shock, I guess."

On the ladder-back chair José stirred, and the boot fell to the floor. His head rose higher. *"Gracias—muchas gracias,"* he said, and he was José Gonzales again, the quiet little man whose ancestors had come into the big land with the early conquistadors and who clung now in this Yankee-invasion time to his one remaining piece of small, sparse valley on the western edge of the Slash Y range and there scratched out a living for his family with a few chickens and a garden and a few goats and a rare willing-ness to haul firewood the long way into town on his one old burro. "I theenk there was snow," he said. "I theenk I fall from the horse." He smiled a small, apologetic smile. "I be dead, no?"

"Not no," said Monte. "Yes. Oh, my, yes, yes. . . . Sunfish, I reckon he's ready to eat. That is, if Chet left him anything."

Silence in the big old room, warm and cheerful, as three men watched the fourth finish the last of the stew, the last biscuit, and his third cup of coffee. José leaned down to set his cup on the floor and pick up one of the boots. *"Gracias,"* he said. "I theenk I go now."

"Whoa there, José," said Monte. "You ain't going no-wheres. It's colder'n an icehouse outside. Snowing to beat hell."

José, bent over, boot in hand, looked at Monte.

"Damn it!" said Monte sharply. "I ain't going to cart you in a second time."

José let the boot drop and sat very still, looking into the fire.

"You're beat up, and that horse of yours ain't got much," said Monte. "Tell you what. When this thing lets up, I'll ride over with you."

José sat very still, looking into the fire. *"Los niños,"* said José. "I theenk I go." He picked up the boot.

"Two women," said Chet softly. "And a couple of kids. José, have they got food and firewood?"

"Un poco," said José. He picked up the other boot.

"The hell with him," said Monte, rising and striding to the window to look out into the swirling grayness.

"Can't let him go like that," said Sunfish. "Hey, Chet, ain't Cal's bearskin somewhere around?"

"Must be," said Chet, pushing up from the armchair and heading for the closed door of the left side room. "And he sure could use some socks."

"Give the fool one of our horses," said Monte savagely, without turning from the window. "But I ain't having a thing to do with it."

Five minutes later José stood in the center of the room, a shapeless small bulk in a long, old bearskin coat that came down to his ankles, an old pair of Cal Brennan's gloves, cap on head with the piece of toweling down over it and his ears and tied under his chin.

"Ain't he something?" said Sunfish. "Looks like a mangy he-bear with mumps."

"I nevair forget," said José. He started toward his burlap bag by the door, and Monte Walsh, leaving the window in long strides, was in the way.

"You damned little gamecock," said Monte bitterly. "You really set on it?"

"Sí," said José simply. *"Los niños."* He shrugged. "Ees

Chreestmas." He started around Monte, but was stopped by a lean, hard-muscled arm clamped over his shoulders. Monte drew a deep breath and looked across the room at Chet.

"All right, Monte," said Chet. He sighed. "Looks like it's us again."

"And me," said Sunfish Perkins. "Maybe you two can take care of José. But somebody's got to take care of you."

Out through the gate, from the partial protection of the high-railed first corral into the swirling snow and wrenching wind, four men, bundled thick against the cold, led four saddled horses.

"Shucks," said Monte Walsh, hefting the half-full burlap bag. "This thing's mighty puny. Rest of you wait a minute." He strode off, carrying the bag with him to the bunkhouse. Inside he lighted the lantern on the old kitchen table.

"What do you think you're doing?" said Chet Rollins from the doorway.

"I got two pair of socks I ain't ever wore," said Monte, heading for his bunk and squatting to reach under. "And a deck of cards that's almost new."

"Whatever for?" said Chet.

"For this bag," said Monte. "Ees Chreestmas."

"Darned if it ain't," said Chet, watching Monte pull a box of checker men from under Dally Johnson's bunk and a mouth organ from under Powder Kent's pillow. "I got a pair of spurs I ain't used yet," Chet said, heading for his own bunk. "And some tobacco I been hiding from you."

Two minutes later the bag was two thirds full. "What they really need is food," said Chet, picking up the lantern and leading the way out and over to the cookhouse. Inside he took an empty burlap bag off a chopping block in a corner and, with Monte helping, began to stuff it with cans from the cupboard nearly filling one end of the room. He stopped. He was looking at two humped objects under limp, well-washed floursacks on the shelf by the stove.

"Now wait a minute," said Monte. "Don't go getting foolish complete."

"Ees Chreestmas," said Chet, taking the larger of the two objects out of its pan and wrapping its flour sack around under it.

"Aw, hell," said Monte. "You're going to be so smart, do it right." He picked up the other object.

Far out in the storm-clogged darkness of night four men on four tough cow ponies, sleet-crusted beyond recognition, slugged through snow up the side slope of a long ridge. Monte Walsh in the lead on a leggy dun peered from under the rim of his pulled-down hat, picking the way. Behind him Chet Rollins on a thick-necked black rode close beside José Gonzales, shrunken down inside the old bearskin coat on a short, sturdy roan. And behind them came Sunfish Perkins, a big, solid shape on a rangy bay.

As they came out on the bare-swept crest, the wind beat at them, and they dropped down the other side. The wind was less brutal here, rushing past overhead. Monte stopped, and the others pulled up with him to breathe the horses.

"He's doing it on nerve alone," said Chet. "But he's doing it."

They pushed on, and José dropped his reins and took hold of the saddle horn with both hands and clung to it, head down. Chet leaned over and grabbed the trailing reins, leading the roan close in beside him, and Sunfish Perkins closed in on the other side. Steadily they pushed on, following Monte's lead.

The swirling snow slackened some, and vision lengthened, and out of banked snow ahead rose the top rails of a rickety corral with an open-end shed at one end and a burro a dim shape in it, and beyond that a low, three-room adobe house.

They stopped by the corral, and Chet pulled José out of the saddle and set him on his feet. Chet took one arm and Sunfish the other, and they moved toward the house. Monte unlooped two burlap bags from saddle horns and followed.

"Hello, in there!" shouted Chet. He began stomping and shaking to get rid of crusted snow. "Hello, in there!" he shouted again, and the door opened. In the doorway stood a woman with a blanket wrapped around her and up over her head, eyes peering out bright and frightened at them. Behind her they could see in the light from a small fire another woman, standing by the fireplace, wrapped in a shawl, an old single-shot rifle in her hands. The first woman backed away as they pushed forward. "*Madre mía!*" she said. "José!"

"He's all right, ma'am," said Chet quickly. "Just wore out mucho trying to get home. Some rest is all he needs. That your bedroom over there?" With the woman leading, he and Sunfish took José through the inner door to the right.

The other woman had set the rifle somewhere. She had looked at each of them in turn and now looked past Monte out the open front door. "Dobe?" she said.

"Shucks, no, ma'am," said Monte, reaching back with one foot to close the door behind him. "But if he'd known about this storm, he'd of sure been here. Now where'll I put these things?"

She pointed to the left inner doorway. Bags cradled in his arms, Monte strode over to the doorway, into it and stopped. Dimly he could make out a mattress on the floor, close to a wood stove in which the remains of a fire still glowed. On the mattress, from under the edge of a ragged quilt, two small heads, stocking-capped, peered up at him. "*San* Nicholas," said one in an awed whisper, and both of them ducked down under the quilt.

Monte looked down at the old quilt and the tiny quiverings that marked two small shapes beneath it. Carefully he stepped over a corner of the mattress and set the two bags against the wall. Carefully he stepped back, still looking down. He began to back out through the doorway and whirled, startled. The other woman had been close behind him.

In the faint light from the fireplace he saw her face, tired and sagging in the relief of long waiting over, smiling at him. "*San* Nicholas," she said softly.

"Aw, shucks, ma'am," said Monte, embarrassed. "Kids say the silliest things." He fidgeted. "I got to go unsaddle that horse José rode," he said quickly. "José can swap him back for his pinto first good chance he gets." Monte fled to the door and out.

The snow had stopped now, and high overhead the wind sighed long and seemingly mournful. Monte strode to the corral and led the roan into the open-end shed and the low nickering welcome of the old burro. He removed the saddle and looked around in the near darkness. "Where's the hay?" he said. "Ain't he got any?"

Something tickled his nose, and he looked up. A few wisps showed sticking through the cracks between the poles of the roof. He strode outside and reached up and pulled from the conical pile covering the roof poles a plentiful supply and a cascade of snow. He scooped up a double armful and took it in. He stood watching the horse and the burro start on the hay, feeling weariness creep along his muscles in the absence of motion. "My, oh, my," he murmured. "Kids sure are crazy sometimes."

From over by the house came a new sound, and he hurried toward it. In the lee of the end wall, where the snow was thin, Sunfish Perkins had scraped a bare spot and pulled there a batch of dead piñon trunks from a pile nearby and was working on them with an old rusty ax. "They ain't got much in there," he said. "Grab yourself a load."

Monte bent over, picking up stove lengths, and moved toward the house and met Chet coming out for more of the same.

Ten double trips later they stood in the central room surveying a shoulder-high stack ranked along the wall between the fireplace and the corner. "That ought to hold 'em for a spell," said Sunfish.

Scuffling sounds came from the room to the right. José Gonzales, thin and meager and indomitable in patched long underwear and a pair of Cal Brennan's socks, struggled into the doorway with two women trying to hold him back. He pulled free and braced one hand against the doorjamb and stood straight. His head rose, erect and somehow dignified. "*Señores,*" he said. "Thees ees your house."

"That's mighty kindly of you, José," said Chet quickly. "Sometime maybe. But we got a ranch to think of. We got a break in this storm too."

"Get back in that bed," said Monte. "Ain't you been fool enough for one night?" He turned. "Come on, let's scat."

Out by the corral three men swung up on three tough cow ponies and headed for the horizon. And back at the house a woman with a blanket wrapped around her stood in the doorway and watched them go. "*Vayan con Dios,*" she said softly.

* * *

34

Far out beyond the ridge wind whistled in long, fierce sweeps, blowing the brittle snow into drifts belly-deep on the three horses slugging patiently through them, needing no guidance, driving straight for the home corral. The bay led, the black followed, and the leggy dun moved in sturdy stride behind. No more snow fell, but the cold was steadily deepening.

Monte Walsh caught himself toppling slowly forward in the saddle. He shook himself vigorously. "Watch it," he muttered. "That's bad." He tried to wriggle his toes inside his boots. There seemed to be no feeling in them.

He looked ahead and saw Chet Rollins swaying some, catching balance in jerky movement. He slapped spurs to the dun and came alongside Chet. "Wake up!" he shouted. "Get down and walk!" He looked ahead. The big body of Sunfish Perkins, hunched down, was rocking slowly forward, jerking back, rocking forward again.

"You too," muttered Monte. He slapped spurs again and was alongside Sunfish. "Snap out of it!" he shouted.

Sunfish's head turned slowly. "What's eating you?" said Sunfish drowsily.

"Damn it!" said Monte, reining in the dun, forcing his reluctant body to swoop down so he could take the reins of the bay close by the bit and yank the horse to a stop. "Tired and cold," he said. "Hell of a combination. Get down and walk!"

"Yeah," said Sunfish. "Reckon you're right." He climbed down and started to shuffle forward, leading the bay.

Monte turned back. The black had stopped. Chet sagged in the saddle, blinking at him. "What you stopping for?" he said drowsily.

"Good gosh!" said Monte. He dismounted and in one furious heave yanked Chet out of the saddle. "Give out on me now," he said grimly, "and I'll bust you one you'll remember." He yanked Chet up to his feet. "Ain't you got ears? I said get walking!"

Monte took the reins of the black and put them in Chet's hand. He turned Chet forward and gave him a push that sent him stumbling ten feet through the snow, the black jerking on the reins and stepping out to follow.

"Keep moving," said Monte. He took the reins of the dun and moved up by Chet and reached out to push him again. He moved up and pushed once more.

"Quit that," said Chet, standing straighter and moving under his own power. "Keep it up, and I'll try kicking your teeth in."

"That's the talk," said Monte. "But just keep moving."

Silent in the great white cold of distance fading away across the long miles into distance, three men leading three horses in single file pushed forward, intent on the effort of driving one foot ahead of the other through the resistant snow.

Monte Walsh felt the blood moving in his legs, lean energy building again in hard muscles of his body. He looked ahead and saw that the same was happening to the others. He saw the big barrel body of Sunfish Perkins smashing steadily through the drifts, breaking trail. "My, oh, my," he murmured. "I'd never tell him, but that sure ain't lard he's packing on that carcass of his."

Cold had crept into the main room of the old ranch house. The fire in the fireplace had dwindled to a few faint embers. Sunfish Perkins, still bundled, knelt in front of it, whittling shavings over the embers from a piece of piñon with clumsy stiffened fingers on the knife. Monte Walsh was lighting one of the lamps. Chet Rollins, finishing shedding his jacket and hat and the bandanna that had been tied over head and ears under it, was starting to unfold blankets and lay them on the mattresses.

Chet stopped, then straightened. Slowly he picked up his jacket and started to put it on.

"Hey," said Monte. "You locoed?"

"We ain't fed the horses," said Chet.

"Think I'd forget that?" said Monte. "Why'd you think I ain't stripped down? Just thawing out a little first. You get busy with those beds."

He pulled up his jacket collar, slipped on his gloves, and went out the door. Down by the first corral he looked through the rails at the dark shapes crowding close, expectant, and began counting. "Six and Sonny took one and left his," he muttered, "and Sunfish brought in seven, and José swapped even." He nodded and went to the barn and pushed open one of the protesting doors. "That thing ain't going to be fixed soon," he said, and went on in, reaching with experienced hands in the dark to pull down a bale of hay. He carried it out by the rails, slipped off the twin cords, and heaved it over, a half at a time.

He leaned on the rails, looking through at the horses jostling one another to get at the hay. Suddenly he pushed out and returned to the barn and took two battered pails from nails on a beam and lifted the lid of a big, tin-lined wooden bin and dipped the pails in. One weighing heavy in each hand, he went out to the corral and in through the gate and to a trough along one side and emptied the pails into it, scattering the contents along the full length. "Come and get it," he said. "You're too stupid to know, but it's a Christmas present."

He watched the horses catch the meaning of the rattle of the pails they drifted over, crowding one another. He

37

saw the pinto, coming late and wary, ease in between two others. He saw the smallish, neat sorrel approach cautiously and slide in too. "When I wake up," he said, "if I ever do, maybe there'll be some more." He left the corral, dragging his legs, and moved up to the house.

Inside, Sunfish Perkins sat on the hearth out of range of a now-healthy fire, slumped back against the fireplace, head dropped sideways, snoring in steady rhythm. Chet Rollins sat in the remnants of an armchair, head nodding, but still awake, waiting.

"I thought maybe you'd bring that bottle," said Chet.

"Shucks," said Monte. "I'm too tired even to drink. Likely it's froze solid anyways, and the bottle broke, and we'd have to get a pail and thaw it. Come on, let's tuck him away. Take the head. There ain't much in that part of him."

Together they lifted Sunfish and carried him to one of the mattresses and laid him down and spread a blanket over him. "If he dies in his sleep," said Monte, "at least he'll have his boots on."

There was silence in the big old room, except for slight rustlings as two men pulled off each other's boots and one blew out the lamp and both lay down on mattresses and reached to draw blankets up over them. Then there was silence in the big old room except for the outside sound of wind hunting along the eaves and finding no entrance.

Monte lay flat, looking up at the old beamed ceiling. "Know what we'll be doing when we get up?" he said. "We'll be eating beef and beans and riding out to thaw windmills; and if that crust that's starting already on the snow out there gets bad, we'll be hauling feed to a lot of hungry cows."

"Yeah," said Chet drowsily. "That's about it."

Monte raised himself on one elbow to look over at Chet

stretched out flat. "You think I don't know," he said, "you fixed it someway for that brown bean just 'cause I already had one. Well, it kind of got you a bellyful."

"It ain't been so bad," said Chet drowsily. "Somehow, wherever you are, things are always happening."

"Shucks," said Monte. "That just goes to show. That's what I keep telling you. Luck and me, we—" He stopped. Chet was asleep.

Monte lay back and stared up at the shadows flickering between the beams. "*Santo* Nicholas," he murmured. "That's me."

Christmas Day dawned cold and clear over the frozen white wonder of the big land. The first light of the morning sun touched the capped peaks of the mountains to the west and moved down them, pink-flushed, and moved over the badlands at their base and a small valley where a three-room house sent smoke drifting up from chimney and stovepipe and moved on over the long ridge that screened this and other valleys and on across the wide, white miles where the blurred tracks of three men and three horses showed in the snow and moved on to glow softly on the drifted flat roof of an old ranch house where three men slept the deep, dreamless sleep of tired muscles and the simple, uncomplicated assurance that they had done and would do whatever needed to be done.

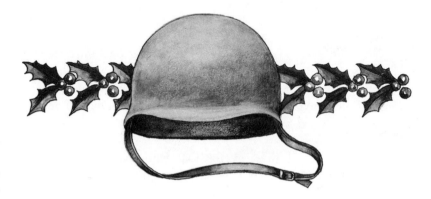

THE ROAD
TO ST. VIVIEN

William Chamberlain

The general's name was Daniel Boone Tucker, but dating to back his plebe days at West Point he'd been known through the service as Old Dan Tucker. The moniker, of course, was a natural. Even now, a few months short of forty, Dan had a perennially youthful face set off by sandy hair inclined to curl. The kid effect was belied by a pair of hard blue eyes and a command of profanity, when Dan was displeased, that was awesome and wonderful to hear.

The Old Dan Tucker tag had been hung on him by a hillbilly roommate named Matthews, and the original Dan Tucker had been a cantankerous man, rough as a cob and justly celebrated in song, so Matthews had claimed. The song had started something like this:

> Get out of the way for Old Dan Tucker,
> He's come to town without his supper.

For some reason that fool refrain kept running through Dan's mind now as the battered truck, towing a shiny new trailer, lurched over the icy secondary track they'd been following ever since the armored car had chased them off the Abomont road.

Old Dan Tucker was going to town darned slow, Dan thought sourly; any minute now he was going to find himself on foot again because there couldn't be much more than a canteen cupful of gas left in the truck's punctured fuel tank. On this little used road he stood a snowball's chance in Hades of catching another ride.

Yet, somehow, he had to get to St. Vivien, still miles to the east across the snowy hills. In St. Vivien was Combat Team Bailey, hard pressed by German assaults from two sides; Dan had to see that Combat Team Bailey held that town, with its vital road center, until the rest of the division could arrive. Maybe that would be tonight, maybe tomorrow or next week. Didn't matter, St. Vivien must hold!

Dan was assistant division commander, and he'd been at the advanced CP at Maugan when the last message had come in from St. Vivien at 0350 this morning. Mark Bailey was dead, so was his exec and one battalion commander. Of the other battalion commanders, one was missing and one wounded. Combat Team Bailey needed help and needed it fast. The radio had gone dead after that.

"Tell Corps I've gone to St. Vivien," Dan snapped to McIntyre, the G-3. "You take care of things here until the Old Man arrives, and get me a jeep and driver!"

McIntyre departed, then returned with his thin face worried. "Sir, Corps thinks you'd better stay here. There are rumors the Germans have reached the Abomont road."

"We won't hold St. Vivien by sticking pins in a map back here!" Dan snarled. "When the Old Man comes up with the rest of the division, tell him to get help to us fast. If St. Vivien goes, we'll have enemy armor sitting in our laps all the way back to Sedan!"

He took off in the predaylight gloom. It was midmorning on the Abomont road when the jeep had skidded, breaking a wheel and the driver's arm and knocking out two of Dan's front teeth. Dan went on by foot, hoping to catch a ride, but traffic seemed to have dried up on this road. Scared of German armor, Dan thought dourly. A little before noon this truck had finally come along. Dan flagged it down, and a sergeant, wearing the marks of an old soldier, thrust his head belligerently out of the cab.

"Well, what do you want, Mac?" he demanded.

"Where you headed?" Dan asked roughly.

"St. Vivien, if it's any of your business," the sergeant said. "I'm lookin' for Combat Team Bailey."

"You'll find 'em there," Dan grunted. "Move over."

The sergeant's name was Ed Peck, and he'd worn the Army's cloth for eight years; but this was the first time he'd ever had to play Santa Claus. The thought of that had been riding him roughshod ever since he and Riviera, the driver, had picked up that confounded trailerful of Christmas stuff in Paris two days ago. Now he wasn't about to take any lip from this little squirt standing in the road with two front teeth out and a muddy snow parka around his shoulders and a stocking cap pulled down around his ears where his helmet should be, by golly.

Dan was reaching for the door.

"Who do you think you are, giving me orders?" Ed Peck demanded. "For all I know you could be a—"

"Tucker's the name," Dan grunted, shoving into the cab. He didn't bother to add his rank. Long ago he'd learned that a man commanded by virtue of his ability to lead and not because of any gadgets on his shoulders. "Get this bucket rolling!"

Peck scowled, toying with the idea of taking this fresh so-and-so down a peg; then he thought better of it. This pint-sized character in the stocking cap had a hard cut to his jaw, and it could be that he was an officer running around loose. Half the fool Army seemed to be doing just that ever since the Germans had busted through the Ardennes eight days ago. Through the years of his service Ed Peck had made a point of letting officers walk on their own side of the street while he stayed strictly on his.

He grunted, "Let's go, Pete," to Riviera, and the truck lurched off, tire chains clanking.

"What's in the trailer?" Dan asked after a little.

Ed Peck gave him a sour look out of the corner of his eyes, wondering if this guy was trying to needle him.

"Christmas presents," he said flatly. "You got any objection?"

Dan didn't answer for a moment. He was thinking. That tears it! Here comes Old Dan Tucker with reinforcements—two soldiers and a load of Christmas mail. That'll scare the bejabers out of von Rundstedt, I betcha!

Aloud he said, "Combat Team Bailey would probably rather have ammo at the moment. It's neither here nor there."

"Colonel Bailey said I was to get this stuff to the regiment by Christmas Eve or else," Peck said stubbornly. "Tonight is Christmas Eve. When we get to Maugan this morning, they say the outfit is at St. Vivien. So now we go to St. Vivien. Got it, Mac?"

"I got it," Dan answered soberly.

No point in telling this sergeant that Colonel Mark Bailey wouldn't be opening any Christmas mail this year, he guessed. They rode in silence, and an hour later they ran into the armored-car patrol. It was scouting ahead of *Panzer Lehr* Division, but they didn't know that or care. It was enough that a spatter of machine-gun fire shot out the windshield and gouged a chunk from Dan's ear and punctured the fuel tank, although they didn't learn that until later, after most of the gas had leaked away. Only the fact that Pete Riviera spotted this secondary road branching to the east through the trees saved their hides. Pete whipped into it, and the Germans didn't follow.

Later, when they stopped to tie up Dan's badly bleeding ear, they discovered that most of their gas was gone. No help for it. They plugged the punctured tank to save what gas was left and continued on. This secondary road wasn't marked on Dan's map, but from the direction it was taking it should come into St. Vivien by the back door, he thought. He'd have to gamble on that because they couldn't go back now.

The truck lurched through a low saddle, and ahead of them the trees began to thin out, showing snowy fields beyond. Riviera blew his breath out in a low whistle of relief.

"Boy, am I glad to get out of these trees," he said to Ed Peck. "They give me the willies!"

"Hold it up," Dan ordered curtly. "I want a look."

Dan dropped to the snow, scowling as the jar set his head to throbbing beneath the bloodstained bandage. He stumbled forward—a bullet at Omaha Beach had left him with a small gimp in his walk—and dropped on one knee at the edge of the trees. Not much to see out there in the gray December afternoon.

The road wound down to where a tiny hamlet made a dark blob against the new snow. A dozen sad houses huddled together with the forlorn look of deserted children. For a moment Dan stayed on one knee, watching for some sign of movement down there among the houses. None came. The people had fled before the advancing Germans, he guessed bleakly. It was a hundred-to-one shot against their finding any gas for the truck down there. Blast it, these people used horses. Well, Dan Tucker was going to get to town one way or another.

Dan had known the war since the Battle of Oran in Algeria, and he had been a colonel when he'd taken a bullet through his knee at Omaha Beach. He'd been await-ing his discharge from the hospital when his star had come, together with orders naming him assistant division commander of a new division arriving piecemeal from England.

> Brigadier General Tucker will proceed to Maugan, France, and there supervise the assembly of advance elements of the division, assuming command thereof pending arrival of division commander.

That had been eight days ago, the same day that von Rundstedt had flung three *Panzer* armies through the Ardennes in what would come to be known as the Battle of the Bulge. A single combat team—Mark Bailey's regiment—reached Maugan four days later when the high brass, desperately seeking to plug a gap in the line, reached back for its last reserves. So Dan sent Mark Bailey, his infantry formations reinforced with odds and ends, to St. Vivien with orders to hold. Dan would have gone with them, but Corps said No.

But now Mark Bailey was done, and Dan had no more reinforcements to send except Dan. So Dan would have to do.

> Get out of the way for Old Dan Tucker,
> He's come to town without his supper.

Back in the truck Pete Riviera talked idly with Ed Peck. "How come the colonel is so set on gettin' that stuff today, Sarge? He want to play Santa Claus?"

Ed Peck knew the answer—the Old Man had told him. "Ed," the Old Man said, "this regiment's green and it's not seen battle and it's scared. That trailerload of Christmas stuff we got in Paris will boost morale a thousand percent. So you go get it."

47

Well, right now it looked like the outfit's morale was going to have to do the best it could without any Christmas mail, Ed Peck thought glumly. Unless that Tucker could come up with a rabbit out of a hat, and Ed didn't think he could. Tucker was beginning to get on his nerves. He wished he knew who he was.

"How would I know?" he said crossly to Riviera's question. "I never figured out why officers do what they do. I think that guy Tucker is an officer, and I don't know what he's doing either."

"Him an officer?" Riviera asked. "If the Army's that hard up, I quit, Sarge. You can give me my time."

"You quit and the Army shoots you," Peck grunted. "Button up that mouth of yours. Here he comes back."

"Village ahead." Dan said, climbing into the cab. "Looks deserted. What's your gas gauge say, soldier?"

"Needle about to fall off backwards," Riviera answered. "Another mile an' the third-class passengers get out and push."

He kicked the engine into life, and they crawled down the gentle grade toward the houses a mile away. Depression was settling into Ed Peck. He didn't like this. He'd heard that low grumble of gunfire ahead, and there was a somber quality in the gray afternoon that worried him. Ed Peck was a good soldier. He'd already fought in North Africa and Sicily, and he wasn't afraid of anything that he could see; but this was different. He had the feeling that something bad was about to happen, and he didn't know what to do about it.

"You an officer?" he asked Dan finally. The urge to know had become too strong. Belatedly he added, "Sir?"

"Yep," Dan said.

"A lieutenant, maybe?"

48

"Nope," Dan grunted.

Ed Peck didn't push the matter further, but for some reason he felt a little better. Through the years of his service he'd become used to the idea that there was a man higher up who knew the answers that he didn't know. The day lost some of its grayness.

Dan sat with his carbine between his knees while he scanned the houses with his hard blue eyes. They passed the first one, its vacant windows looking back at them with an idiot's stare. The truck engine coughed as it began to suck up the last of the gas; its final gasp came opposite a house larger than the rest and set back a little from the road. The snow on its stoop was trampled.

Dan wasn't looking at the house. He'd spotted the two vehicles that were half hidden by a house's far corner— a GI weapon carrier and a jeep, by the Lord Harry! A sudden surge of exultation warmed Dan as he dropped into the snow. "Come on," he said crisply to Ed Peck. "We'll have a look. Could be we've got company here. . . . Cover us, Riviera!"

He led the way up the stoop and hammered on the door. No answer, but he heard the sound of furtive movement within. He slipped inside with his carbine ready and Ed Peck at his shoulder. There was a mussed room, littered with the signs that fleeing people leave: a woman's shawl on a chair, a broken cup on the floor, a kid's torn garment forgotten in a corner. Dan had seen other rooms like it on the road from Oran to Omaha Beach. He had never learned to like them.

A voice called harshly, "Stand still, we got you covered!" It came through a half-open door from a room beyond, a voice with a Dixie accent.

"Come on out. We're Americans," Dan said.

49

"Maybe you are an' maybe you ain't," the voice retorted suspiciously. "There's plenty Germans runnin' around in GI suits. Give us a name if you got one, bud."

"Tucker," Dan said through his teeth, biting at the words. "Either come out or I come in after you!"

A big man, carbine in his hands, appeared in the doorway, a half dozen others at his back. "Tough, ain't you?" he said. "Now you wouldn't be the Tucker that sang for his supper, would you, bud? Danged if you don't look little enough to be."

With a start, Ed Peck recognized the man. Butch Gallery. They'd been sergeants together back at Benning in Forty. He'd never cared much for the guy: Gallery was the bullying kind with a streak of meanness in him. He'd later transferred to the quartermasters and got a commission, Ed had heard. Heard right, it looked, because Gallery wore a lieutenant's bar on his helmet now.

"Never mind about the supper," Dan Tucker was saying. He stood with his carbine in the crook of his arm while he inventoried the little knot of men with hard eyes: stragglers! "Any gas left in those vehicles outside?" he demanded.

"Who wants to know, Dad?" Gallery asked, slouching forward. His eyes were mean and calculating behind the dirty stubble on his face as he looked down at Dan. "Suppose you start showing a little respect around here. You see that bar on my helmet, huh?"

"I see it," Dan grunted. He said over his shoulder to Peck, "Tell Riviera to check their gas, split it evenly among the three vehicles, Sergeant. We're all going to St. Vivien."

Ed Peck yelled the instructions from the stoop, then slipped back into the room. There was going to be trouble here. Most of these birds had weapons in their hands.

They were with Butch Gallery, and Butch could be bad in a fight.

Gallery had lifted the muzzle of his carbine until it covered Dan, but there was still a heavy-humored condescension in his voice as he spoke. "You ain't takin' no gas, Dad," he said. "You're just shaggin' your tail out of here before I—"

Ed Peck hadn't thought that a man could explode so fast. Dan jumped across the half dozen feet that separated him from Gallery. The muzzle of Dan's weapon dug into Gallery's belly, doubling the big man over with an explosive grunt. Then the carbine hit Gallery's cheekbone with the sound of a hammer hitting a barrel. Gallery sat down abruptly on the floor, his weapon slithering away, and Dan swung his look, bright and wicked as an ax blade, on the others.

"A fine pack of tramps!" he said, slamming his words at them like bullets. "Hiding back here like dogs with your tails between yours legs. Line up! Either you start being soldiers again as of now, or I'll make you wish you'd never been born!"

For a moment they shuffled their feet uncertainly, their eyes dropping before the rapier stare of this little character with the bloody bandage showing beneath his stocking cap. Then they slowly ranged themselves into a rough order. Butch Gallery was getting to his feet, blood trickling through the stubble on his face.

"You're goin' to pay for this," he said hoarsely. "I got witnesses that you assaulted an officer an'—"

"Mister," Dan said softly, "are you still worrying about that bar of yours? All right, we'll match rank."

He yanked the muddy parka back, and Ed Peck, watching from one side, saw the gleam of the single star on Dan's collar. Well, I'll be, he thought. An' I asked him if he was a lieutenant! How was I to know? I figured all the generals were back in Paris. Just the same, he was feeling a lot better about things.

"Any stragglers in the other houses?" Dan asked sharply. Gallery, his eyes glazed with shock, mumbled that he didn't know. Dan wheeled on Peck. "Check, Sergeant. If you find any, assemble them out in the street. If anybody refuses to come, shoot him! That's an order!"

"Yes, sir," Ed said. Then he added, "General!"

There were others in this town, all right. Peck tallied them as they lined up in the snow a quarter of an hour later—twenty-seven, counting those who'd been with Butch Gallery. All but three had their weapons and some ammo left. One had a BAR; that pleased Ed Peck as he swung about and saluted and made his report to Dan.

"Good," Dan said. "What about gas?"

"We got enough to get all of us to St. Vivien, sir," Ed answered. "Maybe a little to spare."

Dan Tucker nodded and moved up to stand spraddle-legged in the snow as he let his hard stare run along the faces of the men before him, tired faces, faces needing a shave, faces with eyes set too far back and still haunted by the chaos of the past days. He had to jolt these men out of the apathy into which they had sunk, Dan knew. No ordinary pep talk was going to work a miracle inside men who had descended far into the pit of despair.

"Give me your attention," he said, and the ranks stiffened a little under the confident authority in his voice. "St. Vivien is about six miles east of here. An infantry regiment is holding that town because St. Vivien must be held. That regiment has been catching it for four days and four nights now. It's a green regiment. This is its first battle, but it's got guts and it's hanging on."

He paused for a moment to let his words soak in. I just

hope it's still hanging on, he thought. The men in front of him were listening—that was all, just listening. He dropped his voice to a lower note now and went on.

"Tomorrow's Christmas," he said, switching his subject abruptly. A faint interest showed in the faces of his listeners as he jerked his head toward the trailer. "That trailer's full of Christmas mail from home for those guys who've been taking it on the chin for four days at St. Vivien. Any of you who think you're tough and mean and gutsy enough to help me deliver that Christmas mail, step up and join Task Force Santa Claus!"

It had caught them off guard, Dan saw; he was pleased. They'd been prepared for the old, tired every-man-must-do-his-duty routine; that Santa Claus caper—kid stuff—was an antidote for the stark tragedy that had been their diet up to now.

A pint-sized infantryman wearing a muddy overcoat too long for him grinned. "That straight dope, General?" he asked. "You really got Christmas presents in that trailer?"

"Nothing but," Dan said.

"Doggone, back home they used to say I was too skinny to be a Santa Claus," the doughboy said. "Guess I'll go along."

Dan could feel the mood of these men beginning to change. It wasn't that they cared much about Christmas or St. Vivien or Dan Tucker. Rather it was that here was something, remembered from better days, that they could tie to. It was security of a sort.

Another man moved up. "I always played Santa Claus for my kids," he said in a faintly apologetic voice. "It wouldn't hurt to sort of keep my hand in."

Butch Gallery was the last to move up. Why he did it, he didn't know. There didn't seem to be anything better to do. Anyway, he'd like to see how generals operated.

53

"Load up," Dan said. "Let's hit the road."

The afternoon was dying as the little column climbed toward a notch in the ridge that lifted a low rampart ahead. Here ranked firs screened the crest and ran away in a dark funeral procession to the left. Dan, in the jeep at the head of the column, signaled a halt and went forward on foot to have a look from the notch. Some sixth sense, born of bygone battles, warned of trouble ahead.

Enough light remained to show Dan another shallow valley. Three hundred yards below was a wooden bridge over a small stream that was flanked by trees; a thousand yards beyond was a town with a crisscross of roads—St. Vivien! Dan's heart jumped a little as he heard the distant thump of a machine gun, a heavy and solid sound. It was the sound of an American machine gun; the town still held!

"Good boys," he said under his breath. "Good boys!"

But the sixth sense still nagged him, and now Dan saw why. Something moved among the trees to the left of the bridge, and his straining eyes finally picked out the squat silhouettes of three German tanks; supporting infantry would be with them, he knew, as he swore softly. So the enemy had slipped a force around here to the west, had they? They meant to get into the town by the back door! Well . . . .

Dan spat through the gap in his teeth, and his eyes took on a harder glint as he assessed the terrain and made his plan. He'd move Task Force Santa Claus north under the cover of the woods; the ridge curved to the east, and it would bring them within a couple of hundred yards of the German rear. He'd have enough fire power to create a momentary diversion at least. And, while the Germans were still off balance, he'd send Ed Peck and Riviera across the bridge with the truck and a message to whoever was commanding in St. Vivien.

Dan scrawled that message now on a pad held on his knee.

Am engaging German tank-infantry force thousand yards due west of town. Take steps to counter if necessary. Rest of division now moving up to support you. Good luck and Merry Christmas.

TUCKER, B.G.

That ought to do it, he decided, and started back.

Sergeant Ed Peck, his face faintly worried, was waiting at the jeep, and Dan told him to dismount the men—assemble them here. They came through the fading light, and Dan sketched the thing out for them with clipped sentences; it wasn't good, he knew, but he made no attempt to make it sound better than it was.

"We'll draw the tank fire away from the bridge to let Peck through," he said. "Then we'll play it by ear. Any questions?"

Gallery was the one who spoke. "You mean you want us to fight tanks with rifles?" he asked in a hoarse, incredulous voice.

"Unless you've got a bazooka in your pocket," Dan said grimly. "Peck, as soon as you hear the tank guns open, hightail it for the town. Give this message to whoever's in command and tell him I said to hang on. Help's on the way. Understand?"

"Sir," Ed Peck murmured, "if it's all the same, I'd rather go with the general. Riviera can take the message."

Dan started to refuse, then changed his mind. "So," he said softly, "you don't want to miss the fun. OK, Sergeant."

"Much obliged, sir," Ed Peck said.

He ought to be feeling bad about this, Ed was thinking. The scheme was crazy, one that could kill them all, and he had rocks in his head for staying. Yet somehow he didn't feel bad. Maybe it was because of that iron-butted little character with two teeth gone and that fool stocking cap down around his ears.

Dan had turned back to his handful of waiting men. He could feel the reluctance that ran in them; they were scared. He didn't blame them for that. He was scared too.

He said on a sudden impulse, "This'll be no picnic. Any man who doesn't want to come can ride with the truck."

Then for a moment he waited, knowing the rash gamble he had taken. He relaxed and put a hard grin onto his face as the line stood fast. He checked his carbine and slung it from his shoulder. "Looks like I got a rough bunch in Task Force Santa Claus," he murmured. "All right, follow me!"

It was almost dark when they reached the north end of the woods. Dan deployed them there; he passed the word to hold fire until he gave the command. The tanks were still where he had spotted them earlier, and infantry made little clots around them now. It looked as though the Germans meant to launch their attack on the town as the last of the light faded. Well, time to open the ball.

"Ready," Dan sang out harshly. "Fire!"

The ragged volley stirred the echoes, and surprise multiplied its weight a hundredfold. By the bridge a man yelled in guttural alarm; confused shouting grew as Task Force Santa Claus slammed its bullets into the shadows down there. Dan heard the growl of tank engines, and a rapier of flame split the twilight. Then the clap of the bursting shell was a giant handclap in Dan's ears.

Two more spurts of orange flame lighted the woods, but something was wrong here. Dan swore bitterly as he saw the shells burst far to the right. Riviera had burst out of the notch too soon. Now the truck was bucketing down the slope, trailer swaying crazily behind, as the shells pursued. Rage made a dull red glow in Dan as he found that he was getting to his feet, going down the slope at a gimping run. A voice, his own, was loud in his ears. "Come on, Santa Claus! Who's going to town with Old Dan Tucker? Come on! Come on!"

They came. Dan could hear their feet pounding behind him and their high yells merging with his own. Butch Gallery's voice was there, the voice of the little infantryman in the too-long overcoat, the voice of the man who used to play Santa Claus for his kids. But it was the thing that they were saying, in a sort of crazy chant, that surprised Dan the most. It rose savagely.

"Lay off our Christmas presents! Lay off!"

It was crazy and it wasn't war and it had no right to succeed. But it did. The audacity of this charge was a wicked cutting edge that slashed down everything that stood in its way.

Battle exploded beneath the trees as men stabbed with bayonets or gun muzzles and chopped with gun butts while the tanks churned futilely, impotent in this hand-to-hand melee. A rifle flamed in Dan's face, and he felt the hot kiss of a bullet against his cheek as he swung his carbine, heard the grunt as his man went down. A dull blow struck him in the side, and he staggered; then Ed Peck was beside him with a steadying arm until he got his balance.

"Get their grenades!" Ed was yelling. "Chuck 'em down the tank hatches! Butch, give me a hand!"

Numbness was spreading through Dan's side now, and he knew the blow he'd felt had been a bullet. Off to the left the squat shadow of a tank suddenly belched fire from its ports. Flames began to gut another tank as Dan's knees went soft and he slid down against a tree. Ed Peck came back, stalking big in the gloom.

"General," he was calling. "You OK?"

Dan tried to say, "I'm OK," but the words just wouldn't come.

It was over presently. The last of the German infantry scattered, the German tanks dead. But it had taken a price. Butch Gallery had made up for his meannesses, never feeling the bullet that killed him. The infantryman in the too-long overcoat was gone, a dozen more. Of those that remained, there was not one without a wound. Ed Peck told Dan that, kneeling beside him in the dark.

"A good fight," Dan murmured, as he closed his eyes. "A good fight. I'll sleep a little now."

Sun was coming through a window as Dan opened his eyes. He tried to move, but his side was stiff with bandages. Two men were looking down at him, he saw. One was the Old Man; and Dan knew, thankfully, that the rest of the division had come. The other man was Ed Peck. Dan was glad that Ed was there.

"Thanks for the Christmas present, Dan," the Old Man was saying gently. "You gave St. Vivien to all of us."

Dan thought that over. Today was Christmas. "Task Force Santa Claus gave you St. Vivien, General," he said, and then managed a tight grin. "Old Dan Tucker just came to town for the ride!"

Somehow Ed Peck liked that. It was just the sort of thing he'd expect Dan to say. The doc promised that Dan would be around and as good as new in a few weeks, and Ed Peck already had made up his mind that he meant to do the rest of his soldiering with Old Dan Tucker. A smart sergeant could pull a string or two.

"Merry Christmas, General," Ed said.

BARREN CHRISTMAS

Olaf Ruhen

It was just four days to go to Christmas when the flood began, and I guess you wouldn't believe what a heartbreak it is to have a flood at Christmastime, especially at a Christmastime when everybody was working so hard to make it good. We wanted to make this Christmas something special, because of the way Dad was feeling about Tommy. The day the rain started I had been working on Christmas all my spare time, pretty near.

Just after lunch I saddled up old Stone and rode up into the hills. Stone was nowhere in the same class as my blue roan, Tempest, either for style or for speed, but he had been bred up in the Blue Mountains, and he was as sure as a wallaby among the rocks. Tempest, if anything, was a bit too long in the pastern.

I rode right up to the tops of the hills, looking for where the best Christmas bush was growing, and I gathered a big armful, real bright-red stuff, on long branches. Mum always said you couldn't have an Australian Christmas without Christmas bush, but she didn't know what was coming up for us that year. I rode home the long way, by the swamp, and the Christmas bells were like a carpet—red and gold lilies so bright and thick they were like an acre of flames. And last of all, just a little way from home, I went aside to follow along the banks of the creek, because I wanted to mark a she-oak good enough to serve for a Christmas tree.

There aren't any pines in our part of the country, but the she-oaks look like the real thing when they are young; only they grow out all on one side, and you have to pick one very carefully if you want a good one, and then, sometimes, you have to stand it near the corner after all.

I was away all afternoon, and just as I came to the garden fence near the house and dropped the Christmas bush over it, the rain came down—great big splashes of rain that spread as big as saucers where they hit the clay road in front of the stables.

Ralph was at the trough with the team. He started to ask me how far I'd had to go for the Christmas bush. He liked to get up in the hills himself, but since Tommy had left he hadn't had that much time. But Dad saw him from the door of the smithy, where he was working. (We made all our own hinges and iron gear, and our gates swung better than anybody's.)

"You hurry up and get the team fed," Dad said. "And, Dave, get the cow in. Then you can turn Stone out in the back paddock, against the Hundred Acre."

"Aw, gee, Dad," I said, but he had gone back to the forge. The back paddock meant a half-mile walk.

"The river's going to rise," Ralph told me. "The radio's carried flood warnings all afternoon."

We didn't say anything about Dad getting on our backs like that. He had been a bit touchy and hard to get on with ever since Tommy left home. It began when Tommy came home from school and announced that he wasn't going to have anything to do with the farm. He wanted to study for the Air Force and be a pilot, and he had to get Dad's permission because he was only seventeen. There was a big row, and Tommy left and got a job with a radio store, and Dad was hurt, because he had been counting on Tommy. He took it all out on Ralph. Ralph was a bit slow. He could do anything at all with the stock, but he just didn't have any notion when it came to business, while Tommy was as sharp as a tack. I guess Dad thought I was too young to take much account of. I was only thirteen then, last August. Ralph and I had the same birthday, only he was seven years older.

"What's the use of a peacetime soldier?" Dad used to say. "Walking around in smart uniforms looking at the girls,

Olaf Ruhen

and the rest of the country going to the devil for the want of manpower."

I got soaked to the skin getting Daisy into the byre, and while I was milking her, the rain was making big splashes like little teapots in the pools in the yard, although it had been dry only half an hour before. Then I had to take Stone down to the back paddock. There wasn't much shelter there, up on the rise, but the lower paddocks near the river weren't safe in a flood.

All night the radio was giving flood warnings, and before I went to bed the last warning said that the peak of the flood, racing down the river, would reach Singleton next day at noon.

"That's four in the afternoon for us," said Dad, and he reached forward in his armchair and knocked out the dottle from his pipe. "Good thing it will be daylight," he grunted.

We were sitting on the wide veranda, and I was helping Mum paint a little cut-down barrel for a tub for the Christmas tree. Ralph was plaiting kangaroo hide for a bridle—he had tanned the hides himself in an old copper—and Gran was just sitting. We couldn't see out into the night at all. It was just driving storm.

"Do you think it'll catch the house?" asked Mum.

Dad said, "Could be. I don't think it can be as bad as last time. I think where they put up the embankment for the new road last spring will help to turn the water against the other side of the valley. Anyway, we've never had it bad enough to send us out of here. And the stock will be safe."

"Your father built this house," said Gran. "He built it strong and true, and he had an eye for every risk." She was sitting back in her chair with her arms folded, and her face was in the shadow, but I knew she was looking way back behind the rain and behind the hills and remembering. "This house will be safe from floods," Gran said. "Your father thought of everything. That's why he would never rest till he bought the Hundred Acre at the top of the rise, though it was the poorest land of all."

"Poor enough," said Dad.

Woondibone—that's the name of our place—faces on the river, and there are four hundred acres of flat, rich bottom-land. From there on, the land slopes up, and on the other side of the valley, where it lies to the sun, there are vineyards, but on our side the slopes did not catch the sun just the same way, and we had six hundred acres of them under sheep. The house is near the foot of these slopes, half a mile and more back from the river, and behind the house is the end of a long, gravelly ridge, running right back toward the hills, and cut through with three or four little gullies that feed the creek on the other side. That's our Hundred Acre. We've always called it that; it has no other name. There's also a lot of the run stretching right back into the hills, but it's poor land, still under second-growth bush, with a little heavy timber in the deep gullies. That's where we run the beef cattle and the young horses and the dry sheep, the wethers and store hoggets, and any beasts that are spelling for a while.

"I've got a beauty of a tree picked out," I told Mum, when we had finished painting the tub. "It's super."

"I'll bet you have," she said. "Am I going to get any Christmas bells?"

"I'll fill a dray," I promised her, and she laughed.

I was just going to bed when a flash announcement came through on the radio, with another flood warning:

"At eight-twenty-five tonight—forty-five minutes ago—floodwaters in a crest fifteen or twenty feet high burst levees at Georgetown, where citizens, police, and an Army detachment were filling sandbags. Casualties are feared. Further details are not available but will be announced as they come in. Meanwhile—"

Mother looked up anxiously. "It's a bad one," she said. "First thing in the morning, we'll shift all the stock up to the Hundred Acre, Ralph," Dad said.

I said good-night to them all then and went to bed.

We'd had the flood in the house before. It came halfway up the table legs. We had shifted all the carpets and the rugs and all the furniture that mattered into the attic rooms. The water stayed in the house a day and a half, and when it went down, the smell was something fierce. But if it didn't worry Dad it didn't worry me, and I went to sleep soon with the rain on the roof.

When I woke up the next morning, the rain was coming down harder than ever. The river had risen, and it covered the bottom paddock. Dad and Ralph were there, working with a mob of sheep caught on a little rise around the three old gum trees near the riverbank.

The sheep were panicked, and they wouldn't swim to the other side of the water. Dad and Ralph were wading waist-deep, catching the sheep and bringing them, one at a time, back to the dry land near the house. Rab and Spot, our two heading dogs, were helping them; Rab by the gum trees with the men, holding the mob while the sheep were caught, and Spot holding the safe mob on our side. I dressed as quickly as I could and went down to help. Mum called me back and sent a basket of food with me, because they had had no breakfast.

The water was creeping up all the time, thick brown water. The whole surface of the water was covered with spiders and beetles and big sugar ants and mantises and every other kind of insect you could think of. I had my feet bare, and near the edge the centipedes were squirming over them, racing to get away from the flood. They didn't bite, but I kept a lookout for the spiders, because there are poisonous kinds here that are quite deadly.

Every time they came across with another sheep, Dad and Ralph brushed off the spiders that had climbed up their legs for safety.

"I'll give you a hand," I offered, while they were eating the sandwiches.

"It's a bit deep for you," Ralph said. So I said I'd get the cow in and milk her after breakfast.

When they started to eat, we were standing on dry ground, and when they had finished, the water was up to my ankles.

Well, we worked all morning. I don't think I ever worked so much before. It rained and rained, but it was warm and we didn't mind.

After lunch I thought of something. I thought the river would be backing up the creek, and if I wanted that Christmas tree, I had better hurry. So I took a tomahawk and went out to get it. And when I found it, the tree was standing in a foot of water.

I was away about three hours, I suppose, because I had to go around the long way and I was on foot, and the tree got a little bit heavy, even if it was only about seven feet tall. But I thought they'd be pleased that we had a tree for Christmas after all; only when I came back Dad roared at me.

"Where the devil have you been?" he shouted. "You stay close to the house! And what the dickens do you think you're going to do with that damn-fool rubbish?"

I felt sore about that. If I'd been a kid I'd have felt like crying, because I thought he'd like me to have remembered the Christmas tree. Still, it made Mum happy. Hardly any bigger than me at all, she put her arm around my shoulders.

"Your father's worried, Dave," she said. "He doesn't really mean it." And then she looked at the tree. "Oh, it's a lovely tree," she said. "I think it's the best we've ever had."

I thought so too, and I got the tub and wedged the tree in it tight with bricks and stones. Then I covered them over with earth and covered the earth with she-oak needles I had brought for that. It looked as if it was growing there.

I was still looking at it when Dad came running into the house and called for me to give him a hand, and we started shifting things into the attic rooms. Mum and even Gran came running too. But we had only rolled up the carpet off one floor when the water came up into the house. Dad said he had seen it coming down the valley like a wall. He and Ralph had shifted all the stock into the Hundred Acre by that time; everything outside was safe, and now Ralph had gone off somewhere.

We worked like mad, and we got the attic rooms crammed with things: the drawers that held the linen first, and some of the smaller furniture. We were still working when it was growing dark. I had a Christmas present for Mum and one for Dad, but I hadn't bought the others yet, because this was the day for my allowance, and I hadn't enough money before. Still, I sneaked those two up the stairs without anyone seeing me, and I hid them under my shirts in the drawer. Mum had the oil-burning cooker we used for camping on a stand near the attic windows, and she was making something for us to eat.

Just before dark, Ralph came down off the hill. He waded right up to his neck in water, and then he had to swim a hundred yards. When he came to where the garden had been, he walked again, but the water was up to his armpits, and the current was running strong, just as it does in midriver.

Dad waited till he got in, and then be bawled him out too.

"Hell of a time to go off on your own," he said. "Might have had a chance to save something if you'd been here! Where were you anyway?"

Dad didn't usually swear like that. He was hurt and sore and worried.

"Nicholson's stock were up against the fence," Ralph said. He looked as though he didn't have a care in the world, and I guess that made Dad madder. "I cut the wires and let them into our Hundred Acre. Then I went around, and Peters was having trouble. I cut the wires there, too, and then I gave him a hand for a while. He's lost stock. Lost a lot of it."

"Hasn't Peters got high ground of his own?" Dad asked. He didn't really want Ralph to tell him. He was mad clear through. "There's not more than a scratching of feed for our own stock on the Hundred Acre. What the dickens do you think we're going to feed them on? Suppose we have to keep them there a week?"

"They're neighbors," Ralph said.

I didn't like Dad talking like that. I went out and down the stairs again. It was up near my shoulders on the ground floor, and it was dark and the water seemed cold now and there were wriggly things in it. I felt my way out on the veranda, and the tree was there in its tub; only you couldn't see the tub. I grabbed it by the branches and tried to pull it, and it came easily in the water, so I worked it round through the doors and back to the stairs. I got it up the first four stairs all right, but then the tub was half out of the water, and it got mighty heavy.

I was pulling at it and I fell, and the tree fell with me,

Olaf Ruhen

and I must have made some sort of a noise, I guess, because Dad came down then.

"For heaven's sake, we don't want that kind of rubbish up there," he said. "We haven't got room to move as it is. Haven't either of you boys got any sense at all?"

He yanked me up the stairs by the scruff of my neck, and then he went on talking about Tommy being stubborn, and Ralph being stupid, and me a bit of both of them rolled together. Even eating didn't make him feel good. Mum made a pretty good job of the meal, considering.

Twice—once early in the night and once after midnight —it stopped raining, and there was a break in the clouds. We had no electricity now and had to use storm lanterns, and we couldn't hear anything on the radio, and the water came higher and higher on the stairs. Outside, when the moon came out, the current raced on both sides of us. Once a tree hit the house, and the whole place shook.

The tree hit us with the butt first, and then swung around. It stayed against the wall, and Ralph climbed out —Dad made him put a rope around his waist—and walked it along so that it would go free into the current. Dad was holding the lantern out, and Mum screamed. I looked out and there was a fat old tiger snake draped around the branches. Ralph put his bare foot just a few inches from its head, it looked like, but the snake just stayed there, weaving a little bit, its tongue darting in and out.

Farther out in the current there was stock going down the river. The beasts were all swimming—cattle and pigs mostly, only a few sheep—but they were all swimming with the current, and we didn't think there was much hope for them. There was a little flock of ducks swimming against the current, but they were going downstream too. In among everything there were big clumps of water hyacinth broken adrift; they looked like little forests racing down to the sea.

I went to sleep, but Ralph wakened me. It was still dark, although there was a little light coming, and I knew there was only one more day to Christmas Eve. When I went past the head of the stairs the Christmas tree was standing on the landing with its top branches sticking out of the water. Ralph must have gone down after I went to sleep and brought it as far as the landing.

There was water on the attic floor now, and Dad and Ralph wanted us to shift onto the roof. It didn't seem as if the flood could come any higher—it didn't seem as if there could be that much water in the world—but if it did, they said we musn't be trapped inside the attic. They had rigged up the trestle table so it was half out the attic window, and you could climb on it and step back on the roof at the gully between the two gables.

We all climbed out, and then they put the trestle across the gully of the roof for Mum and Gran to sit on, and Ralph went back and got rugs and a cow cover and all the tinned food and the stove, and we made a little camp on top of our own roof. Dad pulled down the wireless aerial and made a kind of stay with it, and we draped the cow cover over it, because it was still raining, and sat there in that little tent.

But before I came out of the window I got the two little flat parcels that were my presents for Mum and Dad and brought them with me, tucked inside my shirt. Gran was rocking back and forth on the edge of the trestle table, with her feet hanging down in the gully, and Mum was comforting her.

When it was light we could see how bad the flood really was. The Hundred Acre was like a big long island now, and it was crowded with stock—horses and cows and sheep everywhere. They were all restless, and the cows were bellowing and the sheep were bleating. They didn't race about, but they stood nervously, the horses holding their heads high. I could see Tempest and Stone. And I could pick out all the Peters horses and Nicholson's, and there were some I had not seen before. And in one corner there were three kangaroos, and there was a fox lying near them. The dogs were not in sight; they must have been on the other side of the hill. Normally we would have to ride right back into the hills and beyond, ten miles or more, to see a kangaroo, and they were not too plentiful even there. But here were all these animals, and none of them interfering with any of the others.

Out in the current there were dead animals floating down now among the living. The trees that stood out of the water and the electric-light poles were covered with spiders and little lizards and beetles, and some of the trees had snakes in the branches. There wasn't anything to do but just look at the water, and everything we looked at was something else to worry about. Mum kept talking of the neighbors who lived on the lower levels. Every now and then she'd say, "I wonder if the Tullys had much warning," or "The Smiths had just finished painting the house," or something like that.

"Nobody had much warning," Dad said. What he meant was, nobody thought it was going to be so bad. But every flood had been worse. Every flood had brought down the silt and made the river shallower, and it made things worse for the flood to follow.

The water was still creeping up a little—about four inches every hour, Dad said.

About ten o'clock we saw a little boat come around the farthest point upriver, about a mile away. It looked like the old boat Jim Tully used for fishing or duck shooting.

It was made of old iron on a wood frame, and you had to keep bailing it all the time. He just used it in the swamps; it wasn't safe enough for the river.

"Jim's mad to take that thing out," Dad said. "I don't know what he's thinking about."

But I could tell by the way the rower was using his paddles that it wasn't Jim Tully. And I knew who it was.

"It's Tommy!" I shouted. "Tommy's coming!"

Nobody said anything, but they all stood up. Mum had her hand at her throat, and when the little boat twisted and swirled in the current, she looked like Death. But it came fast. It was half full of water when Tommy brought it up, heading it straight for the house. He wedged it in the gully right in front of the trestle table and stepped out on the roof, grinning as though he had just put it up on the bank of a creek.

"How's everybody?" he said.

"Could be worse," Ralph told him.

"Why did you come, Tommy? It was risky," Mum protested.

"Thought I might be useful," said Tommy. "Things are bad, Dad. They don't expect it to go down for three days. Still raining in the headwaters. I thought you might have trouble. The rescuers are out, but it may be days before anyone gets here. I've been on the road since the day before yesterday."

He had an old jersey on and rolled-up trousers and bare feet.

"You must have something to eat," Mum said, pumping the oil stove.

"Tully might have needed his boat himself," Dad said.

Tommy's face sobered. "Bad news about the Tullys," he said. "Old Jim's gone. He didn't have time to make the house. He climbed the haystack, and the haystack went.

71

No other news of him. They brought in all the little Tullys and Mrs. Tully—got them off the roof. I remembered about the boat. It was sunk, of course. I waded in and cut the rope where it was tied to the post near the road."

"Can we go back in the boat?" I asked him, but Tommy shook his head.

"Not a chance. That current must be running ten knots."

"At least we can get over to the Hundred Acre," Ralph suggested.

"That was my idea," Tommy said.

It took hours to get over, one at a time, with another one rowing, and then to bring over all the gear stacked on the roof. It was late afternoon when we had finished. There were airplanes flying over all the time, little spotter planes and a seaplane and two or three of the Big Air-Force bombers. I saw Tommy looking up at them. Tommy always looked as though he had a sight of heaven when he saw an aircraft. I noticed Dad frowning, but nobody said anything. Tommy had always stopped work to look at any plane in the sky, and Dad had always hated it. He hated the Air Force anyway. He had been a prisoner of war at Regensburg when the RAF bombed the place, and his chest was all scarred with flying road metal from a bomb burst. But I think he felt it worse that Tommy didn't like the farm better.

We got a fire going when we reached the Hundred Acre, and with the rain stopped we had a chance to get dry. The Peters family were there too. They had come over in a raft, the three of them, the father and mother and Shirley, who was only ten. And they didn't have anything to eat. They had brought nothing at all except a white cockatoo in a cage, and the cockatoo was driving everybody mad saying, "Hallo, hallo" and "Cocky wants a drink" all the time. We had to share some of our rugs and the tinned stuff. Gran was feeling very sick. She was just lying wrapped up in rugs near the fire.

Only about half the Hundred Acre was out of the water, and there were so many cattle it was already trampled and muddy, so there wasn't anything for the animals to eat. When it came night, the cattle bellowed softly all the time, just standing in one place with their heads low and moaning softly every now and then. There were snakes and lizards everywhere, but we didn't kill them. We just left them. If it was good enough for the fox and the kangaroos to sit quietly, it was good enough for us, Ralph said.

"A lot of this stock won't last three days," Dad said next morning. "There's not going to be any feed when the water goes back either. All that mud. They might have had a chance without these other animals." The Peterses had their own fire, and he was speaking softly. They wouldn't hear.

"While there's life there's hope," Ralph said cheerfully, and he began to whistle. Dad didn't like that either.

But Gran struggled in her blanket and moved as though she wanted to sit up, and Mum ran to help her. She started to cough then, and Mum soothed her and wanted to make her comfortable, so she could lie down again. But Gran said, "Leave me. Let me be."

She looked at Dad and said, "Your father would have been ashamed to hear you, and on Christmas Day. Look you here," she said, "we spent our first Christmas under a tree, your father and I—in a wagon under a tree—and little as we had, it was there to share. I never thought to hear the day a lad of mine would grudge his neighbors a bit of help, and on Christmas Day."

"It's not Christmas Day, Gran," I told her. "It's Christmas Eve."

"It's Christmas Day," she said, stubborn with her great age. "It's Christmas Day for Ralph. It's Christmas Day whenever you're thinking of other people and not of yourself. If you're not happy, it's not a Christmas Day, and if you're thinking of yourself, you're not so happy." She looked confused and pulled the blanket around herself and lay down.

Mum sat at her back with her arm over her. "Gran's sick, poor thing," she said, but Gran never stirred.

We had no water, and the brown flood water was thick and muddy. Ralph got an old drum, and he and Tommy filled it at the edge of the flood and stood it up so it would settle, and we could maybe boil some off the top. But there was nothing we could use straightaway, and we were thirsty.

And then Mum found that Gran was fevered and hot. We worried then. She was very old and very tired, and she had had a hard time in the two nights—nearly three— of the flood.

But about ten o'clock that morning a Navy helicopter swung low over the hill, and we all jumped up and waved. The pilot had a loudspeaker attached to the helicopter somewhere, and his voice came booming down. "If you can hang on another twenty-four hours, hold up your right hands!" it said.

I held up mine and the others would have too, but Tommy yelled, "No!" and pointed to Gran. Then we all pointed to Gran, and straightaway the helicopter began to come down.

Tommy nudged me and shouted something, and his eyes were shining, but I didn't know what he was saying, for the noise was terrific under the rotor blades. The helicopter settled down, light and easy.

A man came out of the machine, and they lifted Gran

in, her eyes big and wide, as though she were frightened. And then Tommy said something to the man. They went off, the big eggbeater lifting into the air with a sort of leap and Tommy looking after it with his eyes lifted and his hands on his hips. Gran raised an arm to us, and that was the last we saw.

Dad was happier now. "That's one worry off our minds," he said.

"Worries never last long," Mum told him.

"Neither does tobacco," he said. "I'd sure feel happier if I could fill the old pipe." That was something I hadn't noticed. Dad had no tobacco in his pipe. When everything looks different, you don't notice some one little thing. I felt under my shirt for his present. It was still there, alongside Mum's, and I pulled it out and gave it to him.

"Merry Christmas, Dad," I said. "I wanted to keep it for the right day, but I guess you might like it today."

He looked at me and said, "Oh, Dave," in a soft kind of way. He unwrapped it, and it was a new leather tobacco pouch, same as I thought he might like. I wondered and wondered whether to spend more money and fill it for him in the store, and then I thought it would look better filled, and thank goodness I bought the tobacco as well.

"It doesn't look like Christmas, but I think there's a feel of it in the air," he said. He picked me up and swung me high, same as he used to do when I was a little kid.

I thought of something else, and I asked him, "Dad, can we have a Christmas tree for tomorrow?"

He laughed and looked around. There weren't any real she-oaks on top of the hill, of course, but there was a little gum tree, the biggest of a group, about ten feet high.

"We could use that one," I said.

"We haven't got anything to put on it, son," Dad said. But we didn't have the tree in the tub anymore, and we didn't have the Christmas bush or the Christmas bells; and there weren't going to be any presents, only what I still had for Mum; and there wouldn't be any Christmas dinner or anything; and suddenly they all seemed to see it my way, and we began to get the tree ready for Christmas as well as we could. We cut away all the other saplings and left this one gum tree standing by itself, and it was a lovely little tree, with the first blossoms it had ever had crowning it.

We just stood and looked at it then. There was some horsehair caught in the fence, and Dad said, "You're not going to get my tobacco back to hang on it, because it tastes so good. But I'll hang this instead, just to show it should have been there."

And he tied the wrapping paper into a little bundle and hung it on the end of one of the branches. And I hung Mum's present on another. Then everybody tied handkerchiefs and bits of stones and sticks and things everywhere, and it looked really a bit like a Christmas tree, even if it was a kind of Christmas tree that nobody had ever seen before. Every stick and stone stood for a present from one to the other, and we invited the Peterses to share the tree, and they hung things on it too—the little Peters girl put both her hair ribbons there.

Late in the afternoon one of the big Air-Force bombers came over and circled the hill. The back door in the fuselage was open, and Tommy ran to Dad, very excited.

"Move the stock back!" he yelled. "It's the feed!"

Dad didn't ask him then. He and Ralph and I ran at the stock, shouting and waving our arms, trying to send them to the other end of the hill so that there would be a clear patch left at our end. The bomber had circled and was coming back, and everybody was down holding the stock back.

"I asked the helicopter pilot," Tommy said. "I told him we needed stock food. This is the feed arriving."

The bomber was overhead now, and three bales of hay came flying from the open door. It circled again, and again three bales came out. We were all on our feet, staying back. I don't know why I watched it all so carefully. I saw the third lot come all the way down. I saw the bale hit the Christmas tree and break it off.

The last bundle was a bundle of blankets, and in the blankets, wrapped up, were parcels of food and tablets to purify the floodwater for drinking and dozens of little things we hadn't known we'd needed.

"What about your peacetime Air Force now?" said Tommy. "What about them?" He was nearly crowing.

Dad put his pipe in his mouth and said, "You win. A fellow can't be expected to know what he's talking about all the time, can he?" He was happy because the stock could be fed.

Ralph was looking at all the things wrapped in the blankets. "Plenty of folderols to hang on the Christmas tree now," he said.

"But there isn't any tree," I said.

I felt mighty sick about it too. I wanted that tree, and that old bale of hay could have landed most anywhere else in the Hundred Acre.

Ralph ran his fingers through my hair and said, "Gee, Dave, that's the worst kind of luck."

"It doesn't matter," I said. "I'd rather the stock had the hay." And just then I remembered, and I rushed to the tree where it was lying on the ground. My present for Mum, the little flat bottle of French perfume, was smashed.

Then I started to cry just like a little kid. I thought I was too old to cry, and I reckon I'll remember it because that's the last time I'm ever going to cry, but I couldn't help it then. I was crying when Mum came over, and I showed her the broken bottle. She picked up the stopper.

"I'm going to keep this anyway," she said. "It'll make the nicest kind of a remembering present. You know, I'd have used the scent, and that would have been that, but the stopper I'll put away and keep it always. It's the only thing I'll ever have that will really remind me of this Christmas and how we all were." It sounded silly, but there was a kind sense in what she was saying, and I listened.

"Everything's going to be all right, you know," she said. "Tommy's going to join the Air Force and Dad's going to be proud of him, and you and Ralph and all of us are going to be happy. It's going to be a really happy Christmas for us all."

Dad was near, and he had his back to us, but I think he was listening.

"There wasn't any roof for the Babe in the Manger. His home was somewhere else, and His gifts came from strangers, just like ours have," Mum said. "But that's the Christmas everyone all over the world remembers."

And it might sound silly, but when I look back on it now, that Christmas we spent in the flood last year was the happiest ever.

CHRISTMAS DAY
IN THE MORNING

Pearl S. Buck

He woke suddenly and completely. It was four o'clock, the hour at which his father had always called him to get up and help with the milking. Strange how the habits of his youth clung to him still! Fifty years ago, and his father had been dead for thirty years, and yet he woke at four o'clock, in the morning. He had trained himself to turn over and go to sleep, but this morning, because it was Christmas, he did not try to sleep.

Yet what was the magic of Christmas now? His childhood and youth were long past, and his own children had grown up and gone. Some of them lived only a few miles away, but they had their own families, and they would come in as usual toward the end of the day. They had explained with infinite gentleness that they wanted their children to build Christmas memories about their houses, not his. He was left alone with his wife.

Yesterday she had said, "It isn't worthwhile, perhaps—"

And he had said, "Oh, yes, Alice, even if there are only the two of us, let's have a Christmas of our own."

Then she had said, "Let's not trim the tree until tomorrow, Robert. Just so it's ready when the children come. I'm tired."

He had agreed, and the tree was still out in the back entry.

He lay in his big bed in his room. The door to her room was shut, because she was a light sleeper and sometimes he had restless nights. Years ago they had decided to use separate rooms. It meant nothing, they said, except that neither of them slept as well as they once had. They had been married so long that nothing could separate them, actually.

Why did he feel so awake tonight? For it was still night, a clear and starry night. No moon, of course, but the stars

80

were extraordinary! Now that he thought of it, the stars seemed always large and clear before the dawn of Christmas Day. There was one star now that was certainly larger and brighter than any of the others. He could even imagine it moving, as it had seemed to him to move one night long ago.

He slipped back in time, as he did so easily nowadays. He was fifteen years old and still on his father's farm. He loved his father. He had not known it until one time a few days before Christmas, when he had overheard what his father was saying to his mother.

"Mary, I hate to call Rob in the mornings. He's growing so fast and he needs his sleep. If you could see how he sleeps when I go in to wake him up! I wish I could manage alone."

"Well, you can't, Adam." His mother's voice was brisk. "Besides, he isn't a child anymore. It's time he took his turn."

"Yes," his father said slowly. "But I sure do hate to wake him."

When he heard these words, something in him woke. His father loved him! He had never thought of it before, taking for granted the tie of their blood. Neither his father nor his mother talked about their children; they had no time for such things. There was always so much to do on a farm.

Now he knew his father loved him, there would be no more loitering in the mornings and having to be called again. He got up after that, stumbling blind with sleep, and pulled on his clothes, his eyes tight shut, but he got up.

And then on the night before Christmas, that year when he was fifteen, he lay for a few minutes thinking about the next day. They were poor, and most of the excitement was in the turkey they had raised themselves and in the mince pies his mother made. His sisters sewed presents, and his mother and father always bought something he needed, not only a warm jacket, maybe, but something more, such as a book. And he saved and bought them each something too.

He wished, that Christmas he was fifteen, he had a better present for his father. As usual he had gone to the ten-cent store and bought a tie. It had seemed nice enough until he lay thinking the night before Christmas, and then he wished that he had heard his father and mother talking in time for him to save for something better.

He lay on his side, his head supported by his elbow, and looked out his attic window. The stars were bright, much brighter than he ever remembered seeing them, and one star in particular was so bright that he wondered if it were really the Star of Bethlehem.

"Dad," he had once asked, when he was a little boy, "what is a stable?"

"It's just a barn," his father had replied, "like ours."

Then Jesus had been born in a barn, and to a barn the shepherds and the Wise Men had come, bringing their Christmas gifts!

The thought had struck him like a silver dagger. Why should he not give his father a special gift too, out there in the barn? He could get up early, earlier than four o'clock, and he could creep into the barn and get all the milking done. He'd do it alone, milk and clean up, and then when his father went in to start the milking he'd see it all done. And he could know who had done it.

He laughed to himself as he gazed at the stars. It was what he would do, and he mustn't sleep too sound.

He must have waked twenty times, scratching a match each time to look at his old watch—midnight, and half past one, and then two o'clock.

At a quarter to three he got up and put on his clothes. He crept downstairs, careful of the creaky boards, and let himself out. The big star hung lower over the barn roof, a reddish gold. The cows looked at him, sleepy and surprised. It was early for them too.

"So, boss," he whispered. They accepted him placidly, and he fetched some hay for each cow, and then got the milking pail and the big milk cans.

He had never milked all alone before, but it seemed almost easy. He kept thinking about his father's surprise. His father would come in and call him, saying that he would get things started while Rob was getting dressed. He'd go to the barn, open the door, and then he'd go to get the two big empty milk cans. But they wouldn't be waiting or empty; they'd be standing in the milkhouse, filled.

"What the—" he could hear his father exclaiming.

He smiled and milked steadily, two strong streams rushing into the pail, frothing and fragrant. The cows were still surprised but acquiescent. For once they were behaving well, as though they knew it was Christmas.

The task went more easily than he had ever known it to before. Milking for once was not a chore. It was something else, a gift to his father, who loved him. He finished, the two milk cans were full, and he covered them and closed the milkhouse door carefully, making sure of the latch. He put the stool in its place by the door and hung up the clean milk pail. Then he went out of the barn and barred the door behind him.

Back in his room he had only a minute to pull off his

clothes in the darkness and jump into bed, for he heard his father up. He put the covers over his head to silence his quick breathing. The door opened.

"Rob!" his father called. "We have to get up, son, even if it is Christmas."

"Aw right," he said sleepily.

"I'll go on out," his father said. "I'll get things started." The door closed and he lay still, laughing to himself. In just a few minutes his father would know. His dancing heart was ready to jump from his body.

The minutes were endless—ten, fifteen, he did not know how many—before he heard his father's footsteps again. The door opened and he lay still.

"Rob!"

"Yes, Dad—"

"You son of a—" His father was laughing, a queer, sobbing sort of a laugh. "Thought you'd fool me, did you?" His father was standing beside his bed, feeling for him, pulling away the cover.

"It's for Christmas, Dad!"

He found his father and clutched him in a great hug. He felt his father's arms go around him. It was dark and they could not see each other's faces.

"Son, I thank you. Nobody ever did a nicer thing—"

"Oh, Dad, I want you to know—I do want to be good!" The words broke from him of their own will. He did not know what to say. His heart was bursting with love.

"Well, I reckon I can go back to bed and sleep," his father said after a moment. "No, hark, the little ones are waked up. Come to think of it, son, I've never seen you children when you first saw the Christmas tree. I was always in the barn. Come on!"

He got up and pulled on his clothes again, and they went down to the Christmas tree, and soon the sun was creeping up to where the star had been. Oh, what a Christmas, and how his heart had nearly burst again with shyness and pride as his father told his mother and made the younger children listen about how he, Rob, had got up all by himself.

"The best Christmas gift I ever had, and I'll remember it, son, every year on Christmas morning, so long as I live."

They had both remembered it, and now that his father was dead he remembered it alone, that blessed Christmas dawn when, alone with the cows in the barn, he had made his first gift of true love.

Outside the window now the great star slowly sank. He got up out of bed and put on his slippers and bathrobe and went softly upstairs to the attic and found the box of Christmas-tree decorations. He took them downstairs into the living room. Then he brought in the tree. It was a little one—they had not had a big tree since the children went away—but he set it in the holder and put it in the middle of the long table under the window. Then carefully he began to trim it.

It was done very soon, the time passing as quickly as it had that morning long ago in the barn. He went to his library and fetched the little box that contained his special gift to his wife, a star of diamonds, not large but dainty in design. He had written the card for it the day before. He tied the gift on the tree and then stood back. It was pretty, very pretty, and she would be surprised.

But he was not satisfied. He wanted to tell her, to tell her how much he loved her. It had been a long time since he had really told her, although he loved her in a very special way, much more than he ever had when they were young.

He had been fortunate that she had loved him, and how

fortunate that he had been able to love! Ah, that was the true joy of life, the ability to love! For he was quite sure that some people were genuinely unable to love anyone. But love was alive in him; it still was.

It occurred to him suddenly that it was alive because long ago it had been born in him when he knew his father loved him. That was it: love alone could waken love.

And he could give the gift again and again. This morning, this blessed Christmas morning, he would give it to his beloved wife. He could write it down in a letter for her to read and keep forever. He went to his desk and began his love letter to his wife: "My dearest love. . . ."

When it was finished he sealed it and tied it on the tree where she would see it the first thing when she came into the room. She would read it, surprised and then moved, and realize how very much he loved her.

He put out the light and went tiptoeing up the stairs. The star in the sky was gone, and the first rays of the sun were gleaming the sky. Such a happy, happy Christmas!

THE CHRISTMAS
PRESENT

Gordon R. Dickson

"What is Christmas?" asked Harvey.

"It's the time when they give you presents," Allan Dumay told him. Allan was squatted on his mudshoes, a grubby figure of a little six-year-old boy, in the waning light over the inlet, talking to the Cidorian. "Tonight's Christmas Eve. My daddy cut a thorn tree, and my mother's inside now, trimming it."

"Trimming?" echoed the Cidorian. He floated awash in the cool water of the inlet. Someone—perhaps it was Allan's father—had named him Harvey a long time ago. Now nobody called him by any other name.

"That's putting things on the tree," said Allan. "To make it beautiful. Do you know what beautiful is, Harvey?"

"No," said Harvey. "I have never seen beautiful." But he was wrong, even as, for a different reason, those human beings were wrong who called Cidor an ugly swamp planet because there was nothing green or familiar on the low mudflats that rose from its planet-wide freshwater sea—only the stunted, dangerous thorn tree and the trailing weed. There was beauty on Cidor, but it was a different beauty. It was a black-and-silver world where the thorn trees stood up like fine ink sketches against the cloud-torn sky, and it was beautiful. The great and solemn fishes that moved about the uncharted pathways of its seas were beautiful with the beauty of large, far-traveled ships. And even Harvey, though he did not know it himself, was most beautiful of all with his swelling iridescent jellyfish body and the yard-long mantle of silver filaments spreading out through it and down through the water. Only his voice was croaky and unbeautiful, for a constricted air sac is not built for the manufacture of human words.

"You can look at my tree when it's ready," said Allan. "That way you can tell."

"Thank you," said Harvey.

"You wait and see. There'll be colored lights and bright balls and stars and presents all wrapped up."

"I would like to see it," said Harvey.

Up the slope of the dyked land that was the edge of the Dumay farm, reclaimed from the sea, the kitchen door of the house opened and a pale, warm finger of light reached out long over the black earth to touch the boy and the Cidorian. A woman stood silhouetted against the light.

"Time to come in, Allan," called his mother's voice.

"I'm coming," he called back.

"Right away! Right now!"

Slowly he got to his feet. "If she's got the tree ready, I'll come tell you," he said to Harvey.

"I will wait," said Harvey.

Allan turned and went slowly up the slope to the house, swinging his small body in the automatic rhythm of the mudshoes. The open doorway waited for him and took him in, into the light and human comfort of the house.

"Take your shoes off," said his mother, "so you don't track mud in."

"Is the tree all ready?" asked Allan, fumbling with the fastenings of his calf-high boots.

"I want you to eat first," said his mother. "Dinner's all ready." She steered him to the table. "Now don't gulp. There's plenty of time."

"Is Daddy going to be home in time for us to open the presents?"

"You don't open your presents until morning. Daddy'll be back by then. He just had to go upriver to the supply house. He'll start back as soon as it's light; he'll be here before you wake up."

"That's right," said Allan solemnly above his plate. "He

shouldn't go out on the water at night because that's when the water bulls come up under your boat and you can't see them in the dark."

"Hush," said his mother, patting him on the shoulder. "There's no water bulls around here."

"There're water bulls everyhere. Harvey says so."

"Hush now, and eat your dinner. Your daddy's not going out on the water at night."

Allan hurried with his dinner. "My plate's clean!" he called at last. "Can I go now?"

"All right," she said. "Put your plate and silverware into the dishwasher."

He gathered up his eating utensils and crammed them into the dishwasher, then ran into the next room. He stopped suddenly, staring at the thorn tree. He could not move; it was as if a huge, cold wave had suddenly risen up to smash into him and wash all the happy warmth out of him. Then he was aware of the sound of his mother's footsteps coming up behind him, and suddenly her arms were around him.

"Oh, honey!" she said, holding him close, "you didn't expect it to be like last year, did you, on the ship that brought us here? They had a real Christmas tree, supplied by the space lines, and real ornaments. We had to make do with what we had."

Suddenly he was sobbing violently. He turned around and clung to her. "Not a—Christmas tree—" he managed to choke out.

"But, sweetheart, it is!" He felt her hand, soothing the rumpled hair of his head. "It isn't how it looks that makes it a Christmas tree. It's how we think about it, and what it means to us. What makes Christmas is the loving and the giving—not how the Christmas tree looks or how the presents are wrapped. Don't you know that?"

"But—I" He was lost in a fresh spate of sobs.

"What, sweetheart?"

"I—promised—Harvey—"

"Hush," she said. "Here—" The violence of his grief was abating. She produced a clean white tissue from the pocket of her apron. "Blow your nose. That's right. Now what did you promise Harvey?"

"To—" He hiccupped. "To show him a Christmas tree."

"Oh," she said softly. She rocked him a little in her arms. "Well, you know, honey," she said, "Harvey's a Cidorian, and he's never seen a Christmas tree at all before. So this one would seem just as wonderful to him as that tree on the spaceship did to you last Christmas."

He blinked and sniffed and looked at her doubtfully.

"Yes, it would," she assured him gently. "Honey—Cidorians aren't like people. I know Harvey can talk and even make pretty good sense sometimes, but he isn't really like a human person. When you get older, you'll understand that better. His world is out there in the water, and everything we have on land is a little hard for him to understand."

"Didn't he *ever* know about Christmas?"

"No, he never did."

"Or see a Christmas tree or get presents?"

"No, dear." She gave him a final hug. "So why don't you go out and get him and let him take a look at the tree? I'll bet he'll think it's beautiful."

"Well . . . all right!" Allan turned and ran suddenly to the kitchen, where he began to climb into his boots. "Don't forget your jacket," said his mother. "The breeze comes up after the sun goes down."

He struggled into his jacket, snapped on his mudshoes, and ran down to the inlet. Harvey was there waiting for him. Allan let the Cidorian climb onto the arm of his jacket and carried the great, light bubble of him back into the house.

"See there," he said, after he had taken off his boots with one hand and carried Harvey into the living room. "That's a Christmas tree, Harvey."

Harvey did not answer immediately. He shimmered, balanced in the crook of Allan's elbow, his long filaments spread like silver hair over and around the jacket of the boy.

"It's not a real Christmas tree, Harvey," said Allan, "but that doesn't matter. We have to make do with what we have because what makes Christmas is the loving and the giving. Do you know that?"

"I did not know," said Harvey.

"Well, that's what it is."

"It is beautiful," said Harvey. "A Christmas tree beautiful."

"There, you see," said Allan's mother, who had been standing to one side and watching. "I told you Harvey would think it was beautiful, Allan."

"Well, it'd be more beautiful if we had some real shiny ornaments to put on it, instead of little bits of foil and beads and things. But we don't care about that, Harvey."

"We do not care," said Harvey.

"I think, Allan," said his mother, "you better take Harvey back now. He's not built to be out of the water too long, and there's just time to wrap your presents before bed."

"All right," said Allan. He started for the kitchen, then stopped. "Did you want to say good-night to Harvey, Mommy?"

"Good night, Harvey," she said.

"Good night," answered Harvey, in his croaking voice.

Allan dressed and took the Cidorian back to the inlet.

When he returned, his mother already had the wrapping papers in all their colors, and the ribbons and boxes laid out on his bed in the bedroom. Also laid out was the pocket whetstone he was giving his father for Christmas and a little inch-and-a-half-high figure he had molded out of native clay, kiln-baked and painted, to send home to Allan's grandmother and grandfather, who were his mother's parents. It cost fifty units to ship an ounce of weight back to Earth, and the little figure was just under an ounce, but the grandparents would pay the freight on it from their end. Seeing everything ready, Allan went over to the top drawer of his closet.

"Close your eyes," he said. His mother closed them tight.

He got out the pair of work gloves he was giving his mother and smuggled them into one of the boxes.

They wrapped the presents together. After they were finished and had put the presents under the thorn tree, with its meager assortment of homemade ornaments, Allan lingered over the wrappings. After a moment, he went to the box that held his toys and got out the container of toy spacemen. They were molded of the same clay as his present to his grandparents. His father had made and fired them; his mother had painted them. They were all in good shape except the astrogator, whose right hand—the one that held the pencil—was broken off. He carried the astrogator over to his mother.

"Let's wrap this, please," he said.

"Why, who's that for?" she asked, looking down at him. He rubbed the broken stump of the astrogator's arm shyly.

"It's a Christmas present . . . for Harvey."

She gazed at him. "Your astrogator?" she said. "How'll you run your spaceship without him?"

"Oh, I'll manage," he said.

"But, honey," she said. "Harvey's not like a little boy. What could he do with the astrogator? He can't very well play with it."

"No," said Allan. "But he could keep it. Couldn't he?"

She smiled suddenly. "Yes," she said. "He could keep it. Do you want to wrap it and put it under the tree for him?"

He shook his head seriously. "No," he said. "I don't think Harvey can open packages very well. I'll get dressed and take it down to the inlet and give it to him now."

"Not tonight, Allan," his mother said. "It's too late. You should be in bed by now. You can take it to him tomorrow."

"Then he won't have it when he wakes up in the morning!"

"All right then," she said. "I'll take it. But you've got to pop into bed right now."

"I will." Allan turned to his closet and began to dig out his pajamas. When he was securely established in the warm, blanketing field of the bed, she kissed him and turned out everything but the night-light.

"Sleep tight," she said. Then, taking the broken-armed astrogater, she went out of the bedroom, closing the door all but a crack behind her.

She set the dishwasher and turned it on. Taking the astrogator again, she put on her own jacket and mudshoes and went down to the shores of the inlet.

"Harvey?" she called.

But Harvey was not in sight. She stood for a moment, looking out over the darkened night country of low-lying land and water, dimly revealed under the cloud-obscured face of Cidor's nearest moon. A loneliness crept into her from the alien land, and she caught herself wishing her husband was home. She shivered a little under her jacket and stooped down to leave the astrogator by the water's edge. She had turned away and was halfway up the slope to the house when she heard Harvey's voice calling her.

She turned about. The Cidorian was at the water's edge—halfway out onto the land, holding wrapped up in his filaments the small shape of the astrogator. She went back down to him, and he slipped gratefully back into the water. He could move on land, but found the labor exhausting.

"You have lost this," he said, lifting up the astrogator.

"No, Harvey," she answered. "It's a Christmas present. From Allan. For you."

He floated where he was without answering for a long moment. Finally he said, "I do not understand."

"I know you don't." She sighed and smiled a little at the same time. "Christmas just happens to be a time when we all give gifts to each other. It goes a long way back. . . ." Standing there in the dark, she found herself trying to explain and wondered, listening to the sound of her own voice, that she should feel so much comfort in talking to Harvey. When she was finished with the story of Christmas and what the reasons were that had moved Allan, she fell silent. And the Cidorian rocked equally silent before her on the dark water, not answering.

"Do you understand?" she asked at last.

"No," said Harvey. "But it is a beautiful."

"Yes," she said, "it's a beautiful, all right." She shivered suddenly coming back to this chill, damp world from the warm country of her childhood. "Harvey," she said suddenly, "what's it like out on the river—and the sea? Is it dangerous?"

95

"Dangerous?" he echoed.

"I mean with the water bulls and all. Would one really attack a man in a boat?"

"One will. One will not," said Harvey.

"Now I don't understand you, Harvey."

"At night," said Harvey, "they come up from deep in the water. They are different. One will swim away. One will come up on the land to get you. One will lie still and wait."

She shuddered. "Why?" she said.

"They are hungry. They are angry," said Harvey. "They are water bulls. You do not like them?"

She shuddered. "I'm petrified." She hesitated. "Don't they ever bother you?"

"No, I am. . . ." Harvey searched for the word. "Electric."

"Oh." She folded her arms about her, hugging the warmth in to her body. "It's cold," she said. "I'm going in."

In the water, Harvey stirred. "I would like to give a present," he said. "I will make a present."

Her breath caught a little in her throat. "Thank you, Harvey," she said gently and solemnly. "We will be very happy to have you make us a present."

"You are welcome," said Harvey.

Strangely warmed and cheered, she turned and went back up the slope and into the peaceful warmth of the house. Harvey, floating still on the water, watched her go. When at last the door had shut behind her, and all light was out, he turned and moved toward the entrance to the inlet.

It appeared he floated, but actually he was swimming very swiftly. His hundreds of hairlike filaments drove him through the dark water at amazing speed, but without a ripple. Almost it seemed as if the water were no heavy substance to him but matter as light as gas through which he traveled on the faintest impulse of a thought. He emerged from the mouth of the inlet and turned upriver, moving with the same ease and swiftness past the little flats and islands. He traveled upriver until he came to a place between two islands where the water was black and deep and the thorn bushes threw their sharp shadows across it in the silver path of the moonlight.

Here he halted. And there rose slowly before him, breaking the smooth surface of the water, a huge and froglike head, surmounted by two stubby cartilaginous projections above the tiny eyes. The head was as big as an oil drum, but it had come up in perfect silence. It spoke to him in vibrations through the water that Harvey understood.

"Is there a sickness among the shocking people that drives them out of their senses, to make you come here?"

"I have come for beautiful Christmas," said Harvey, "to make you into a present."

It was an hour past dawn the following morning that Chester Dumay, Allan's father, came down the river. The Colony's soil expert was traveling with him, and their two boats were tied together, proceeding on a single motor. As they came around the bend between the two islands, they had been talking about an acid condition in the soil of Chester's fields, where they bordered the river. But the soil expert—his name was Père Hama, a lean, little dark man—checked himself suddenly in midsentence.

"Just a minute—" he said, gazing off and away past Chester Dumay's shoulder. "Look at that."

Chester looked and saw something large and dark floating half-awash, caught against the snag of a half-drowned tree that rose up from the muddy bottom of the river some thirty feet out from the far shore. He turned the boat wheel and drove across toward it.

"What the devil—"

They came up close, and Chester cut the motor to let the boats drift in upon the object. The current took them down, and the nearer hull bumped against a great black expanse of swollen hide, laced with fragile silver threads and gray-scarred all over by what would appear to have been a fiery whip. It rolled idly in the water.

"A water bull!" said Hama.

"Is that what it is?" queried Chester, fascinated. "I never saw one."

"I did—at Third Landing. This one's a monster. And *dead*!" There was a note of puzzlement in the soil expert's voice.

Chester poked gingerly at the great carcass, and it turned a little. Something like a gray bubble rose to show itself for a second dimly through several feet of murky water, then rolled under out of sight again.

"A Cidorian," said Chester. He whistled. "All crushed. But who'd have thought one of them could take on one of these!" He stared at the water-bull body.

Hama shuddered a little, in spite of the fact that the sun was bright.

"And win—that's the thing," the soil expert said. "Nobody ever suspected—" He broke off suddenly. "What's the matter with you?"

"Oh, we've got one in our inlet that my son plays with a lot—call him Harvey," said Chester. "I was just wondering. . . ."

"I wouldn't let my kid near something that could kill a water bull," said Hama.

"Oh, Harvey's all right," said Chester. "Still. . . ." Frowning, he picked up the boat hook and shoved off from the carcass, turning about to start up the motor again. The hum of its vibration picked up in their ears as they headed downriver once more. "All the same, I think there's no point in mentioning this to the wife and boy, no point in spoiling their Christmas. And later on, when I get a chance to get rid of Harvey quietly. . . ."

"Sure," said Hama. "I won't say a word. No point in it."

They purred away down the river.

Behind them, the water-bull carcass, disturbed, slid free of the waterlogged tree and began to drift downriver. The current swung it and rolled, slowly, over and over until the crushed central body of the dead Cidorian rose into the clean air. And the yellow rays of the clear sunlight gleamed from the glazed pottery countenance of a small toy astrogator, all wrapped about with silver threads, and gilded it.

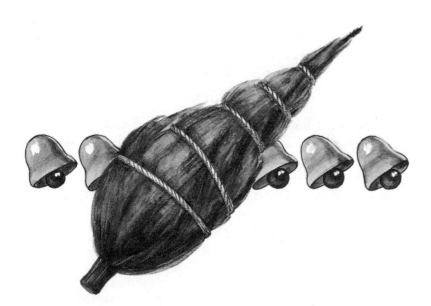

FRANCIE NOLAN'S
CHRISTMAS TREE

Betty Smith

Christmas was a charmed time in Brooklyn. It was in the air long before it came. The first hint of it was Mr. Morton going around the schools teaching Christmas carols, but the first sure sign was the store windows.

You have to be a child to know how wonderful is a store window filled with dolls and sleds and other toys. And this wonder came free to Francie. It was nearly as good as actually having the toys to be permitted to look at them through the glass window.

Oh, what a thrill there was for Francie when she turned a street corner and saw another store all fixed up for Christmas! Ah, the clean, shining window with cotton batting sprinkled with stardust for a carpet. There were flaxen-haired dolls, and others, which Francie liked better, who had hair the color of good coffee with lots of cream in it. Their faces were perfectly tinted, and they wore clothes the like of which Francie had never seen on earth. The dolls stood upright in flimsy cardboard boxes. They stood with the help of a bit of tape passed around the neck and ankles and through holes at the back of the box. Oh, the deep-blue eyes framed by thick lashes that stared straight into a little girl's heart, and the perfect miniature hands extended, appealingly asking, "Please, won't *you* be my mama?" And Francie had never had a doll except a two-inch one that cost a nickel.

And the sleds! (Or, as the Williamsburg children called them, the sleighs.) There was a child's dream of heaven come true! A new sled with a flower someone had dreamed up painted on it—a deep-blue flower with bright-green leaves—the ebony-black painted runners, the smooth steering bar made of hardwood and gleaming varnish over all! And the names painted on them! *Rosebud! Magnolia! Snow King! The Flyer!* Thought Francie, "If I could only have one of those, I'd never ask God for another thing."

Francie Nolan's Christmas Tree

There were roller skates made of shining nickel with straps of good brown leather and silvered, nervous wheels, tensed for rolling, needing but a breath to start them turning as they lay crossed one over the other, sprinkled with mica snow on a bed of cloudlike cotton.

There were other marvelous things. Francie couldn't take them all in. Her head spun, she was dizzy with the impact of all the seeing and all the making up of stories about the toys in the shopwindows.

The spruce trees began coming into the neighborhood the week before Christmas. Their branches were corded to hold back the glory of their spreading and probably to make shipping easier. Vendors rented space on the curb before a store and stretched a rope from pole to pole and leaned the trees against it. All day they walked up and down this one-sided avenue of aromatic leaning trees, blowing on stiff ungloved fingers and looking with bleak hope at those people who paused. A few ordered a tree set aside for the day; others stopped to price, inspect, and conjecture. But most came to touch the boughs and surreptitiously pinch a fingerful of spruce needles together to release the fragrance. And the air was cold and still and full of the pine smell and the smell of tangerines, which appeared in the stores only at Christmastime, and the mean street was truly wonderful for a little while.

There was a cruel custom in the neighborhood. It was about the trees still unsold when midnight of Christmas Eve approached. There was a saying that if you waited until then, you wouldn't have to buy a tree, that "they'd chuck 'em at you." This was literally true.

At midnight on the Eve of our dear Saviour's birth, the kids gathered where there were unsold trees. The man threw each tree in turn, starting with the biggest. Kids volunteered to stand up against the throwing. If a boy didn't fall down under the impact, the tree was his. If he fell, he forfeited his chance of winning a tree. Only the toughest boys and some of the young men elected to be hit by the big trees. The others waited shrewdly until a tree came up that they could stand against. The littlest kids waited for the tiny, foot-high trees and shrieked in delight when they won one.

On the Christmas Eve when Francie was ten and Neeley nine, Mama consented to let them go down and have their first try for a tree. Francie had picked out her tree earlier in the day. She had stood near it all afternoon and evening, praying that no one would buy it. To her joy, it was still there at midnight. It was the biggest tree in the neighborhood, and its price was so high that no one could afford to buy it. It was ten feet high. Its branches were bound with new white rope, and it came to a sure pure point at the top.

The man took this tree out first. Before Francie could speak up, a neighborhood bully, a boy of eighteen known as Punky Perkins, stepped forward and ordered the man to chuck the tree at him. The man hated the way Punky was so confident. He looked around and asked, "Anybody else want to take a chance on it?"

Francie stepped forward. "Me, mister."

A spurt of derisive laughter came from the tree man. The kids snickered. A few adults who had gathered to watch the fun, guffawed.

"Aw, g'wan. You're too little," the tree man objected.

"Me and my brother. We're not too little together."

She pulled Neeley forward. The man looked at them—a thin girl of ten with starveling hollows in her cheeks but with the chin still baby-round. He looked at the little boy with his fair hair and round blue eyes—Neeley Nolan, all innocence and trust.

"Two ain't fair," yelped Punky.

"Shut your lousy trap," advised the man, who held all power in that hour. "These here kids is got nerve. Stand back, the rest of youse. These kids is goin' to have a show at this tree."

The others made a wavering line. Francie and Neeley stood at one end of it and the big man with the big tree at the other. It was a human funnel with Francie and her brother making the small end of it. The man flexed his great arms to throw the great tree. He noticed how tiny the children looked at the end of the short lane. For the split part of a moment, the tree man went through a kind of Gethsemane.

"Oh, Jesus Christ," his soul agonized, "why don't I just give them the tree, say Merry Christmas and let 'em go? What's the tree to me? I can't sell it this year, and it won't keep till next year."

The kids watched him solemnly as he stood there in his moment of thought. "But then," he rationalized, "if I did that, all the others would expect to get 'em handed to 'em. And next year nobody atall would buy a tree off me. They'd all wait to get 'em handed to 'em on a silver plate. I ain't a big enough man to give this tree away for nothin.' No, I ain't big enough. I ain't big enough to do a thing like that. I gotta think of myself and my own kids."

He finally came to his conclusion. "Oh, what the hell! Them two kids is gotta live in this world. They *got* to get used to it. They got to learn to give and to take punishment. And by Jesus, it ain't give but *take, take, take* all the time in this goddamned world." As he threw the tree with all his strength, his heart wailed out, "It's a goddamned, rotten, lousy world!"

Francie saw the tree leave his hands. There was a split bit of being when time and space had no meaning. The whole world stood still as something dark and monstrous came through the air. The tree came toward her blotting out all memory of her ever having lived. There was nothing, nothing but pungent darkness and something that grew and grew as it rushed at her. She staggered as the tree hit them. Neeley went to his knees, but she pulled him up fiercely before he could go down. There was a mighty swishing sound as the tree settled. Everything was dark, green, and prickly. Then she felt a sharp pain at the side of her head where the trunk of the tree had hit her. She felt Neeley trembling.

When some of the older boys pulled the tree away, they found Francie and her brother standing upright, hand in hand. Blood was coming from scratches on Neeley's face. He looked more like a baby than ever with his bewildered blue eyes and the fairness of his skin made more noticeable because of the clear red blood. But they were smiling. Had they not won the biggest tree in the neighborhood! Some boys hollered "Hooray!" A few adults clapped. The tree man eulogized them by screaming, "And now get the hell out of here with your tree, you lousy bastards."

Francie had heard swearing since she had heard words. Obscenity and profanity had no meaning as such among those people. They were emotional expressions of inarticulate people with small vocabularies, and they made a kind of dialect. The phrases could mean many things according to the expression and tone used in saying them. So now, when Francie heard themselves called "lousy bastards," she smiled tremulously at the kind man. She knew that he was really saying, "Good-bye. God bless you."

* * *

It wasn't easy dragging that tree home. They had to pull it inch by inch. They were handicapped by a boy who ran alongside yelping, "Free ride! All aboard!" who'd jump on and make them drag him along. But he got sick of the game eventually and went away.

In a way, it was good that it took them so long to get the tree home. It made their triumph more drawn out. Francie glowed when she heard a lady say, "I never saw such a big tree!" A man called after them, "You kids musta robbed a bank to buy such a big tree." The cop on the corner stopped them, examined the tree, and solemnly offered to buy it for ten cents, fifteen cents if they'd deliver it to his home.

Francie nearly burst with pride, although she knew he was joking. She said she wouldn't sell it for a dollar even. He shook his head and said she was foolish not to grab the offer. He went up to a quarter, but Francie kept smiling and shaking her head no.

It was like acting in a Christmas play where the setting was a street corner and the time, a frosty Christmas Eve, and the characters, a kind cop, her brother, and herself. Francie knew all the dialogue. The cop gave his lines right and Francie picked up her cues happily and the stage directions were the smiles between the spoken lines.

They had to call up Papa to help them get the tree up the narrow stairs. Papa came running down. To Francie's relief, he ran down straight and not sidewise, which proved that he was still sober.

Papa's amazement at the size of the tree was flattering. He pretended to believe that it wasn't theirs. Francie had a lot of fun convincing him, although she knew all the while that the whole thing was make-believe. Papa pulled in front and Francie and Neeley pushed in back, and they

Betty Smith

began forcing the big tree up the three narrow flights of stairs. Papa was so excited that he started singing, not caring that it was rather late at night. He sang "Holy Night." The narrow walls took up his clear sweet voice, held it for a breath, and gave it back with doubled sweetness. Doors creaked open and families gathered on the landings, pleased and amazed at the something unexpected being added to that moment of their lives.

Francie saw the Tynmore girls standing together in their doorway, their grey hair in crimpers, and ruffled, starched nightgowns showing under their voluminous wrappers. They added their thin poignant voices to Papa's. Floss Gaddis, her mother, and her brother, Henny, who was dying of consumption, stood in their doorway. Henny was crying, and when Papa saw him, he let the song trail off; he thought maybe it made Henny too sad.

Flossie was in costume waiting for an escort to take her to a masquerade ball, which started soon after midnight. She stood there in her Klondike-dance-hall-girl costume with sheer black-silk stockings, spool-heeled slippers, one red garter fastened under a knee, and swinging a black mask in her hand. She smiled into Papa's eyes. She put her hand on her hip and leaned seductively—or so she thought—against the doorjamb.

More to make Henny smile than anything else, Papa said, "Floss, we got no angel for the top of this Christmas tree. How about you obliging?"

Floss was all ready to make a dirty reply about the wind blowing her drawers off if she was up that high. But she changed her mind. There was something about the big proud tree, now so humble in its being dragged; something about the beaming children; something about the rare goodwill of the neighbors and the way the lights looked turned low in the halls, that made her ashamed of her

108

unspoken reply. All she said was, "Gee, ain't you the kidder, Johnny Nolan."

They set the tree up in the front room after spreading a sheet to protect the carpet of pink roses from falling pine needles. The tree stood in a big tin bucket with broken bricks to hold it upright.

When the rope was cut away, the branches spread out to fill the whole room. They draped over the piano, and it was so crowded that some of the chairs stood among the branches. There was no money to buy tree decorations or lights. But the great tree standing there was enough. The room was cold. It was a poor year, that one, too poor for them to buy the extra coal for the front-room stove. The room smelled cold and clean and aromatic. Every day, during the week the tree stood there, Francie put on her sweater and cap and went in and sat under the tree. She sat there and enjoyed the smell and the dark greenness of it.

THE CHRISTMAS DOLL

B. J. Chute

It was three days to Christmas and the ice skates and the hockey stick for Miss Martha Jones lay on the top shelf of the front closet, pushed well back and cunningly camouflaged by her father's raincoat.

Marty moved the coat only just enough to assure herself that what lay underneath was what she had ordered, or rather requested. She was not a bossy child, although at nine her skinned-back pigtails, round, freckled face, and solid body gave her a look of confidence that intimidated nervous adults.

Satisfied now that it was safe to boast about what she was getting, Marty climbed down and went into the kitchen where she had left her ski jacket and an apple, then shouted into space that she was going sliding.

Her mother, upstairs with a mouthful of pins, shouted back with muffled good temper that this plan was acceptable and would she please get home in time for dinner.

"What's for dessert?" yelled Marty, weighing her answer.

"Apple pie."

Marty paused in the act of inserting herself into her jacket and contemplated her apple. There would be one apple fewer in the pie, but that was life. "I'll be back in puh-lenty of time," she shouted reassuringly. "Where're my mittens?"

"In your pocket."

This turned out to be quite true, and one of them in fact was fortuitously wedded to a half-sucked sourball. Marty worried it loose and stuck it in her mouth. "Well, g'bye," said Marty briskly, and shot out the door.

She paused to collect her sled, and then, performing "Hark the Herr-uld Angels Sing" at the top of her lungs, she bounced euphorically toward Hudson Hill. It was perfect sliding weather, just cold enough, and she could see her breath puffing importantly before her into bright clear air that smelled of snow and Christmas.

The hill, when she arrived, was swarming with that deceptively aimless activity peculiar to anthills, subway crowds, and children at play. Marty lifted her sled and clutched it firmly to her middle. She then gave a loud cry, somewhat reminiscent of one of the Valkyries on a good day, and shot off recklessly downhill.

The cold air blew in her face and rushed down her throat, her mouth being open to shout "Hallelujah! Hallelujah!" which was happily appropriate to the holiday season and made very good shouting. For a moment she owned the hill, the town, and the whole world, all in one burst of dizzy white speed. No one could fly so fast or so far as Marty Jones, except maybe God's angels. "Hallelujah!" shouted Marty, addressing the angels with heavy reverence. "Hallelu—"

She broke off in midglory, her mouth ajar. The unthinkable had happened. A sled and rider rocketed past her at breakneck speed. Marty gave a violent heave and pressed herself flatter, urging her sled to take wings and meet the challenge, but it was too late although it was a willing sled and would die game.

She arrived at the base of the hill a good two yards behind her competitor and came to a stop by dragging both feet, duck style. The owner of the rival sled rose from his chariot, glistening red and yellow, and stood looking down at her, his hands in his pockets.

He was a new boy she had never seen before—about her own age, chunky, with a button nose and a cowlick of brown hair plastered to his forehead with damp from the flying snow. He said, "Ya-ah," hostilely.

"Yah yourself," said Marty. "Bet you can't steer as good as I can."

113

"I c'n steer rings around you with both hands tied behind my back," he informed her, and, to further show his superiority, he spit grandly through a gap in his front teeth.

She eyed him jealously. "You lose a tooth?"

"Got knocked out in a fight."

This was an advantage beyond all argument. Marty herself had never qualified for a fist fight, since males were always checked by some primeval sense of etiquette, probably batted into them by their mothers, and females refused to fight at all. Marty returned to the attack. "What's your name?"

"Rodney," he said and added, "Anderson," after a pause.

"Rodney's a fatheaded name," said Marty pleasantly. "Mine's Marty Jones."

"Fathead yourself," said Rodney.

The amenities dealt with, they fell into a brief silence. At this moment, a third sled put in a sudden appearance, and its rider fell off into the snow with a resigned cry. It was Tommy Eagan and he always fell off, some inscrutable Providence having shaped him like a butterball without any adhesive surfaces. Like the White Knight, he had acquired a fine ability for talking upside down, whether in a winter snowdrift or a summer blackberry thicket. What he was announcing this time was that Rodney was his cousin.

"Ho," said Marty gratefully, as this information explained Rodney. He was visiting. She whacked snow off Tommy's rear with a brisk mitten and gave him to understand that she and Rodney had already met.

"I beat her coming down the hill," said Rodney.

"You did *not*," said Marty, spirited if inaccurate.

Rodney eyed her distantly. "I'm going to get a new sled for Christmas," he said.

114

"*My* parents," said Marty loftily, "are giving me ice skates and a hockey stick."

"Like fun they are," said Rodney. "Girls can't play hockey."

"Marty can," said Tommy, with his beautiful, rotund loyalty.

Rodney grunted one of those superior masculine grunts that are calculated to drive an independent female mad. It worked fine on Marty. "I'll show you exactly the kind of skates they're buying me," she said, inflating dangerously like a frog or balloon. "They're in the window at Grover's store and they've got rawhide laces and everything. And there's a hockey stick goes with 'em."

"Huh," said Rodney. "My parents would give me anything in your old store window that I wanted, I guess."

"So would mine," said Marty quickly.

"They would not."

"They would so." Her pigtails were not actually sizzling at the ends, but they gave that effect.

Tommy, who had a pacific nature, said, "You can show him the skates on the way home, Marty. We can go round by Grover's."

"I'll just do that little thing," said Marty, and gave herself and sled a flounce that faced them uphill. "Betcha don't dare go down the other side of the hill."

Tommy looked at her anxiously. "Through the trees?"

"Sure, through the trees." She poked a finger at Rodney. "You don't dare."

"I dare anything once."

"Yah, cowardy custard," said Marty. "*I* dare anything twice." She started uphill, her sled following her faithfully. Rodney glared and girded himself for battle.

By the end of an hour, they had arrived at a stalemate. Marty had a wilder way with tree trunks and overhanging branches, but Rodney had a system all his own of streaking straight for peril and then hauling his sled back on its tail like a plunging mustang. Tommy was aghast. Each downhill flight convinced him that it would be their last, and he had carted them off to the hospital and broken the sad news to their parents so many times that at last even his fertile imagination tired, and he sat quietly on his sled like a small, stout, and sympathetic snowman.

Rodney was the one who, with calm superiority, said he guessed Marty must be tired by now, being a girl. Marty's chin jutted dangerously. Tommy reminded them they were going to stop by Grover's. Marty grunted, jerked her sled around, and led the way, while in her vigorous mind's eye she skated victoriously to some distant goal line, wielding her Christmas stick as Rodney labored to catch up, his ankles sagging.

Grover's store shone out at them through the early December twilight. Even from a distance, they could see the Christmas tree in the big plate-glass window, brave with lights and dripping tinsel, the mysterious red-ribboned packages clustered at its base, and that wonderful stardust, plum-pudding, carol-chanting look of anticipation that is both wild and holy and not possible to any other month or any other tree.

Marty inhaled the richness. The skates would be lying near the tree, their glittering runners reflected in its fat red balls. She tasted the flavor of saying casually, "That's the kind I'm getting," then looked and gave a yelp of indignation. The skates were gone, and in their place, crowning frustration, there was a doll.

Marty's eyes, impervious to dolls, skimmed over it and lit on a catcher's mitt, newly introduced and indicating that Grover's was not lost to all sense of decency. If there had been less snow around, she might have coveted the mitt, but her mind was on skates, and baseball could wait for spring. She muttered at the window and turned to scowl at the doll.

It was different from other dolls being neither round, blond, nor vacuous. It had brown hair and a serene look, and it was wearing an old-fashioned dress dotted all over with tiny blue and pink roses. Black-strapped slippers showed just below the ruffle of the hem.

After a minute, Tommy poked Marty with his elbow. "There're your skates," he said. "Back under the tree."

"She's stuck on the doll," said Rodney.

Marty turned around and gave him a look of fury. "I am not! I was looking at a catcher's mitt." The mitt was right behind the doll; it could have been true. It should have been true because Marty despised dolls. She pointed firmly to the skates. "Those are mine," she said.

Rodney admitted grudgingly that they weren't bad.

Marty didn't hear him. She was staring into the window again, and after a moment she pulled one of her braids around and began to chew fiercely at the end. Something inside her was stretching out its arms to the doll, and she felt a dreadful melting-down sensation. She said gruffly, "What'd they want to put a silly old doll in the window for?" and knew in the same instant that she had hurt the doll's feelings.

Dolls didn't have feelings. She must be crazy.

Marty gave a sudden bloodcurdling whoop, whirled her sled around, and announced to the world that the last one back to her house was a black-eared baboon.

Tommy said, "Gee whizz, Marty—" with no more hope of a successful protest than a corporal reasoning with a general, but Rodney had already leaped into action. Marty, who could give two jumps to a jackrabbit, caught up with him at the first lamppost and cut in front of him so neatly with her sled that he fell into a snowbank.

The incident reconstructed her morale and cleared her head of fuzzy emotions so that she forgot the doll. Greatly cheered, she went into the house, which was blooming with lights and the good hot smell of cinnamon and apple.

Her father accepted her large hug placidly and pulled a pigtail. Her mother, apprehended in the kitchen, observed that she was trailing melted snow all over the house and shooed her upstairs. With a comfortable sense of being extremely welcome, Marty shucked off her snowpants in the middle of her room, started to pull off her sweater, and paused on the fourth button.

The doll was back, tugging at her thoughts.

Still unbuttoning vaguely, she went over and sat on the bed. Her room was messy but austere, and there was no place whatever for a brown-haired doll in a rose-sprigged dress.

Well, it could go on top of the bed. It wasn't absolutely necessary to have a life preserver marked S.S. *Algonquin* on her pillow. The life preserver could go under the bed, and the doll could—

"Oh, yah!" said Marty furiously to the empty room. "Yah, yah, yah!" What would everyone think if it got out that Marty Jones was hankering for a doll? That little pipsqueak of a Janie Darrow had told her once to act more ladylike, and Marty had kicked her hard right in the rear of her fancy pink dress. Suppose Janie Darrow saw her with a doll?

She didn't want a doll. She didn't want a doll! She wanted her skates and her hockey stick.

Comforted by her mounting passions, Marty flopped down on the bed. Tonight they would decorate the tree and on Christmas Eve the package with her skates in it would go under the wide branches. With a card, with her name on it. No Santa Claus nonsense. Marty had mistrusted his whiskers from the crisp age of two.

In her mind's eye she began to undo the skates. The red ribbon unwound, the tissue paper pushed aside crackling, the white shiny cardboard of the lid waiting to be lifted. . . . She lifted it.

Inside was the doll.

Marty sat up with a terrible snort and smacked her feet down on the floor. Fugitive from dreams, she hurled herself at her closet, snatched a pair of grubby overalls off a hook, and proceeded to dress herself wrathfully. They were the toughest-looking things she owned, and she felt a vast need for toughness.

She didn't want the doll. She never had wanted a doll, and she never would want a doll. That settled that.

She clattered downstairs to dinner, and the overalls proved their worthiness at dessert time when the apple pie burst its bounds.

Mr. Jones gazed at his daughter in a kind of awe. "What did you do all day, squirt?"

"Coasted," said Marty in a pie-crusted voice. "Tommy Eagan's cousin is visiting him. He *really* stinks."

"Marty." The upward inflection in her mother's voice was a comment on the choice of words.

"Smells," said Marty with refinement. "His name is Rodney, and he thinks he can beat me sliding."

"Ah." Mr. Jones nodded comprehension.

"We came back past Grover's," said Marty, acting under compulsion. "They've put a *doll* in the window."

"Dolls," said Mr. Jones broad-mindedly, "are not essentially vicious."

Marty thought of the brown hair to be stroked, the pink

and blue roses, and the tiny strapped shoes. "Dolls sti—"

"Marty!"

"I don't like dolls."

"Very sad," said her father. "We bought you one for Christmas."

For just a second Marty's heart gave a magnificent leap; then she realized her father was teasing. She subsided into a second piece of pie. It wouldn't have been *the* doll, anyway.

"Marty, you'll bust."

"Are we going to trim the tree tonight?"

"As soon as the dishes are done."

There was always something in the world postponing the ideal. The silverware was lucky to get put away at all, and the moment the drawer closed on it and the dish towel hit the rack, Marty dragged her parents into the living room.

"First, the star," said Marty ritualistically. "The star on top." She held it with reverence. It was five-pointed and silver and sprinkled with bits of tinsel. It was a Wise Man's star, fit to be stationary in a sky of great importance on a night of great light, and Marty always felt a little holy when it finally got into place on top of the tall green tree.

The red balls came next, then the blue, the silver, and last, the gold, trembling and bowing at the tips of the branches. Then the special ornaments: a woolen Santa Claus that Marty didn't like but that had been on Marty's mother's tree when she was a baby and therefore had seniority rights; an angel with gold wings, a halo, and an expression of impressive vacuity; a peacocklike bird of great dignity and poor balance; and, finally, Marty's favorite, a rainbow ball caged in glittering silver and powdered with gold.

"'s gorgeous," said Marty approvingly. "Now the big hunks of tinsel—"

"Hanks," said her father.

"Hanks?"

He translated. "Ropes."

"Hanks," said Marty, always pleased to meet up with a new word. By the time tinsel hung in glittering loops from star to carpet, the whole room was lit up with Christmas. "Every year we do it better," she said solemnly.

She sat down on the floor, hugging her knees and contemplating the star-crowned achievement. On Christmas Eve, her parents would put their present for her under the tree, and she would be allowed to poke it. Even though she knew what was inside, there would be that pleasantly tingling feeling of anticipation. You could get that feeling just looking at the space under the tree where the package would be.

She looked at the space hopefully, and nothing happened. This was one of the best moments of Christmas, and nothing happened at all. Marty rested her chin unhappily on her knees. It wasn't just because she knew beforehand what her present would be; she almost always knew that. And she wanted the skates, she wanted them terribly. Only this morning, she had been in a passion of joy.

She got to her feet, walked over to the tree, and touched a red ball with one finger. It danced, and she gave it another poke, and this time it nearly fell off. She backed away and wandered across the room to the sofa.

The doll rose uninvited in her mind, lovable beyond any reasonable dream. Marty closed her eyes and said, "Nebuchadnezzar," under her breath, exorcising it with strong words, but the doll clung.

She opened her eyes. Throughout her life she had been

all of a piece, and now there was a stranger inside her, a stranger who wanted a doll.

"Darling," said Marty softly, making the doll welcome, ashamed to be saying it and helpless not to.

Someone tapped at the window. She whirled around and saw the tip of a round nose pressed hard against the pane. Armed in the righteousness of invaded privacy, Marty stalked to the front door and yanked it open.

"Hello," said Tommy sociably. "We're going to the store for ice cream. Can you come along?"

"Nope," said Marty. "It's too late. I wouldn't be allowed."

Rodney waded up off the snow-banked lawn and eyed her loftily. "She's not old enough to go out by herself," he explained to Tommy.

"I'm as old as you are!"

"You're a girl."

"Is that so?" said Marty ragingly. "I can beat you running, I can beat you sliding, I can beat you at anything."

Rodney said, "I'm going skiing tomorrow. I'm going down Hudson Hill on skis."

Without stopping to think about it, Marty said, "So'm I."

Rodney briskly told her not to be silly. "You can't ski."

"I can so."

"You can not. Tommy says you don't know how."

"Tommy doesn't know everything," said Marty darkly, implying that she had led a life of great danger in the Alps.

"It just happens," said Rodney casually, "that I'm going to ski down the *other* side of the hill."

Tommy gave a sudden piteous bleat. It had begun to dawn on him that these two were a bad influence on each other. "Don't pay any attention to him, Marty," he said earnestly. "He's kidding."

"Who's kidding?" said Rodney. "I'm not scared of any old hill."

"I'm not either," Marty said quickly. "Anything you can ski down, I can too."

"Huh. You haven't even got skis."

This was true, but her father had a pair. They were in the basement, near the collection corner where she kept various things such as the large bone that her father generously thought might have belonged to a dinosaur.

"I'll take my father's skis," said Marty grandly.

In technical possession of the field, she swaggered back into the house and started upstairs, looking over her shoulder for just a moment at the tree with its trembling shower of tinseled light and the bright glitter of the Christmas balls, reflecting the room in endless enchanting miniatures.

She took the stairs two at a time and sang her way into her pajamas. A general feeling of goodwill, based soundly on the routing of Rodney, enveloped her. Her father's skis would undoubtedly be too large, but that hardly mattered. . . .

Her father's skis.

About to leap heartily into bed, Marty paused and sat down conservatively on its edge. After a moment, she drew her feet in, pulled the covers over her and hunching up, stared at the opposite wall.

She must have been crazy to tell Rodney she would take her father's skis. Suppose she busted them? It was perfectly possible, since she'd never been on skis before. It wasn't going to be much use trying to explain to her father that Rodney had dared her.

What on earth had gotten into her? She'd never done a silly thing like that before, trying to throw her weight around by bragging she could do something when she knew she couldn't. Marty Jones's self-confidence had never needed that kind of bolstering.

There must be something wrong with her, some awful kind of thing happening so that she wasn't Marty Jones any longer, but a stranger. The old Marty might have bragged a little, but not this stupid way. She curled up tight and buried her nose in the pillow.

The whole thing was the doll's fault. She'd only bragged to Rodney to prove to herself that she wasn't the kind of dope who wanted a doll. She hated the old thing. Nothing had gone right since she had seen it in the store window. If she had it here now, she would smash its head.

The image of the doll rose behind her closed eyelids and looked at her pleadingly. Marty hardened her heart. She would have none of it; she would show it she didn't care. Tomorrow, first thing, she would go look into Grover's window, and the doll wouldn't interest her a particle. Not one tiny little measly bit. Deliberately, coldly, she pushed it out of her mind—the flower-sprigged dress, the white hands and the little feet, the brown hair.

After a moment, the destructive catalogue became quite easy, and she felt a sort of sleepy triumph. She would make the doll let go of her, and, with the doll, the stranger inside would let her go too. Rid of them both, she would be herself again.

Her mind drowsed, slid deliciously into a picture of herself on skis, flashing in and out of trees while Rodney stood by in amazement and chagrin. The whole problem began to fade, get misty at the edges, dissolve.

Marty gave a little growl of hope and comfort, rearranged herself, and slept.

There were muffins for breakfast the next morning, and

the Christmas tree looked beautiful. Marty announced that she was going down to the village. "I hafta," she said firmly.

"Well, if you hafta, you hafta," her mother agreed. "Don't stuff yourself so, Marty, the muffins won't get away."

Marty had just pushed a buttery half into her mouth and at the same moment reached for reinforcements. She grinned amiably, impervious to etiquette, and when she left the house she had two emergency muffins in her pockets.

The good crisp air pleased her. She felt strong and confident and superior, last night's optimism and this morning's muffins making a firm foundation inside her. She was Marty Jones with no invisible fidgets.

Grover's came in sight. She put her hands nonchalantly into her pockets, hit a muffin on each side, and pulled one out. Chewing like some calm cow, she advanced on the window. Her eyes swept it with cool detachment and came to rest immediately on the doll, skirts spread, hands neatly folded on rose-sprigged lap.

Marty's heart turned over. She clutched her muffin in helpless love. She pressed her nose against the glass of the window, and, through the frosty O of her breath, the doll's beauty shone steadfastly.

She, who had thought she would never want to see the doll again, could have howled from pure frustration and longing.

A voice said, "Hullo, Marty," and she spun around, choking down adoration and muffin. Tommy and Rodney were behind her, of course; they were following her around. In silent savagery, she began chewing on her second muffin.

125

"What you doing?" asked Tommy.

Marty said distantly, "I had an errand. At the grocery store." She hated them both. They were always making her tell fibs.

"What were you looking at?"

"Nothing," said Marty.

Tommy, who liked speculation, waved an inclusive hand. "If you could have anything you wanted in the window, what would you take?"

It was generally a good game, but this time it wasn't. The doll looked at Marty in a waiting sort of way.

"The catcher's mitt," said Marty stoically. It was like hitting a kitten across its nose, and it was no good telling herself that the doll didn't have any feelings. She glared at Rodney.

He spit through the gap in his front teeth in a business-like way. "When you going to take your father's skis?"

"Right now," said Marty, hating him. She turned on her heel.

"See you at the hill," said Rodney.

Instead of going in shouting by the back door, Marty let herself quietly in through the basement. Completely unadjusted to secrecy, she was clumsy about it, but she had no choice since, if her mother saw her taking the skis, there would be considerable trouble. Marty did not approve of having trouble with parents. They were right in general, and in this case they would be right in particular. It would be hopeless to try to explain.

The skis were heavy, and her feet dragged as they took her to the hill. Maybe Rodney had changed his mind.

He hadn't. He was already there, waiting for her, with Tommy a faithful shadow. The three of them made a silent procession to the other side of the hill. Marty, with Tommy's help, laid her skis out funereally. "They're too big for you," said Tommy.

Marty nodded. The fact seemed like a reproach, a reminder that the skis were not for her. She turned them carefully toward the brow of the hill before she adjusted the bindings and snapped them on. Rodney kept eyeing her impatiently, but it was all right for him. His skis fitted.

Safely mounted, she took her first real look at the hill. Sled-borne, she knew every twist and turn of it, and the trees were no more than a bright challenge. From skis, it looked altogether different. The sudden coldness in her hands was not winter's. She caught her breath and took a quick look at Rodney.

"Scared?" he said.

"In a pig's eye," said Marty, using a frowned-upon expression to stiffen her knees.

"Well, go ahead then."

"Go ahead yourself."

"You don't know how to ski," Rodney pointed out. "I don't want you running into me from behind."

Tommy said, "I don't see why either of you has to go down," but his was a lost cause.

Marty swallowed hard. She shuffled her feet forward and found her knees trembling so they would hardly support her. It was because she was afraid she might damage her father's skis.

She knew hopelessly that it wasn't that way at all. She was just plain scared, the way any sissy would be. The way Janie Darrow, or any silly girl who played with dolls would be. It was bad enough to have shown off by taking a stupid dare in the first place, but to be frightened now was unforgivable.

She was face to face with the true Marty Jones at last, and it was not to be endured. At least, no one was ever going to know that she was scared.

With a fierce cry, Marty thrust herself forward over the brow of the hill.

She heard Rodney's shout. Or it might have been Tommy's. And she saw the tree coming at her, distant and black and narrow for an astonishingly long time, and then suddenly it was so close that the deep-ridged bark was like a map with rivers on it.

If she had been on her sled, she would have known just how to twist and scrape lightly past. But the skis refused to turn, no matter how her feet wrenched at them. The tree refused to move. The map with its rivers became bigger than the sky.

Marty yelled and tried madly to kick off her father's skis so they wouldn't break. The rivers rose up spectacularly. A big, bright, black star exploded with a crash and split itself into a million comets.

The world spun itself quiet.

"Abrasions, contusions, and lacerations," said Dr. Crosby cheerfully.

Even from a great, dreamy distance, Marty recognized his voice and then her mother's saying anxiously, "Is she all right, doctor?"

"My dear Mrs. Jones," said Dr. Crosby, "children are indestructible. Where did you come from, baby dear? Out of the rockpile into the here." He started to make packing-up noises. Marty moved a cautious eyelid. "Stop peering at me, Marty," he said sternly. "Your mother's worried about you. Sit up and show her you're all right."

She sat up and she was all right, except for her head,

which swam. He put a nice, large, cool hand on it and smiled unexpectedly. "All right, Tarzan, lie back again. I'll drop by in the evening, Mrs. Jones. Keep her in bed. If necessary, tie her down."

Mrs. Jones smiled. The doctor departed. After a moment, Marty said, "Mum," in a small voice. "What happened to the skis?"

"One of them broke."

Marty smoothed the top of her sheet with infinite care over the blanket. "It wasn't a very good idea my taking them, was it?"

"I've heard better ideas." However, she gave the blanket a pat, and the blanket included Marty. "Go to sleep now. I'll pull the shades."

Marty slid down against the pillow, closed her eyes, and slept instantly. She woke to a twilit room, sat up in bed, and yelled, "Moth-er!"

Her mother put her head around the door and diagnosed acute recovery. "You've got visitors, Marty. Rodney and Tommy. Do you want to see them?"

"Sure, send 'em in," said Marty regally, and assumed a consciously heroic pose. When the door opened again, Tommy was the one who sidled around the edge, his round face expressing concern. After him came Rodney. Rodney's expression was glum, and he was carrying a box.

Marty eyed it with curiosity. Rodney said, "My aunt says I shouldn't have dared you to go down that hill. She says to tell you I'm sorry."

"'s all right," said Marty, queenlike.

"I brought you a present," said Rodney, still glum, and shoved the box toward her. The words *Grover's Department Store* showed on its lid.

The catcher's mitt, thought Marty. Rodney was the one

who maintained that girls couldn't play baseball. Triumph tasted sweet in her mouth. She broke the string and lifted the box cover.

The doll stared up at her.

It was dearer, more lovely even than she had remembered it. It lay in its nest of tissue paper, smiling gently, its arms reaching out in the serene confidence of being welcome.

Marty's hands followed her heart and reached out too, and then her hands stopped. She couldn't let them go to the doll. Not in front of Rodney.

She pushed the box away from her, not rudely but just enough to show how little she cared. The doll still smiled.

And all of a sudden something inside Marty stretched and grew tall. She knew that she loved the doll and that the doll loved her. There were more important things than having people admire you. Who cared what Rodney thought?

She took the doll firmly out of its box, and, holding it close to her, she looked at Rodney over its head. Her mouth was a tight line and her chin stuck out. Silently, she dared him to jeer at her.

Rodney said, "My aunt picked it out for you. I told her you'd rather have had the catcher's mitt, but she said no." His face was no more scornful than the doll's. "Would you rather have had the catcher's mitt, Marty?"

Marty shook her head. "I like the doll," she said. "I like the doll a whole lot."

He looked puzzled but relieved, and she decided there was no use trying to explain. She loved the doll, and when she got her skates on Christmas morning, under the star-tipped shiny tree, she would love them too.

Loving a doll was simply a new part of herself that she hadn't met before. Marty felt a warm interest in the discovery. It was like opening a package. Sometimes you knew what was inside, and sometimes you were surprised. It was all rather unexpected, like Christmas itself, but, like Christmas too, it was very rich and secure.

She held the doll tight in her arms and bent her head to impress a kiss on the round, sweet cheek. The kiss, however, was interrupted by a novel sensation.

Marty raised her head. "Hey, you know what!" she said happily. "I think I must've knocked a front tooth loose. I'll be able to spit."

She knew her friends would be very happy for her, a girl with a loose tooth and a new doll on the same day.

GREETINGS FROM
A. BLEDSOE SMITH

Irene Kampen

My aunt Clara gives me these crazy presents for Christmas. She gives me pillows with poodle faces that have no stuffing and you're supposed to put your pajamas in them and carry them by the handle to a slumber party. She gives me leather folders with fifty plastic pockets inside that are supposed to be filled with fifty photographs. She gives me autograph books and jeweled lipstick cases with no lipstick in them and scrapbooks called *My Teen Years,* and she gives me wire racks for my phonograph records. Everything she gives me is something you have to put something else into and you wouldn't use in a million years, anyway, empty or full, and I have to write her notes saying, "Dearest Aunt Clara. You think of the best presents! How in the world did you ever know I have been simply longing to start a five-year diary?"

Last Christmas she gave me the weirdest present of all. It was a metal box like the one my mother keeps her recipes in, and it was full of blank filing cards, and the outside was all painted with holly and berries, and it said on it, *My Christmas-Card List.*

"This is the end," I told my mother. "She has gone too far this time. I have stuffed pillows, and I have filed records, and I have pasted in ticket stubs, but I absolutely refuse to set up an index system for my Christmas cards."

"I think it's a lovely gift," my mother said. My mother always says this about everybody's presents and especially Aunt Clara's. Aunt Clara is my father's sister, and since my father passed away three years ago, my mother has been very patient with her. "She has been very thoughtful since Daddy left us," my mother is forever saying. "I think it's extremely sweet of her to remember us at Christmas with such lovely gifts."

"I have an aunt who gives me a pair of socks every Christmas," Ronny said. "They're always size five. She started giving me socks when I was born, and I got a pair this Christmas, and they're still size five."

"Well, I think socks are a lovely gift," my mother said automatically.

It was Christmas morning, and Ronny had come over to see our presents. We had been going steadily since Thanksgiving, because my mother won't let me go steady until I am seventeen. Steadily means you don't go out with anyone else unless someone asks you whom you absolutely can't resist. Steady means you don't go out with anyone else, period.

My mother looked sort of pretty this morning in her new housecoat that I had given her. She had been a little sad when we got up, because we still weren't able to cope too well with Christmas without my father; but after Ronny came over and gave me my present, she got more alert. The present upset her, I guess.

It was a bottle of perfume with a label that pictured a lady fondling a snake. The perfume was called Serpent of Sex. A little gold tag on the stopper said, "Danger!"

My mother was going to say something to Ronny about suitable gifts for fifteen-year-old girls, but he handed her a package for herself, so she couldn't. It was addressed, "To Mrs. Pat Morrison, Alicia's mother," and inside it was a metal sign, made like a license plate, with, "Don't honk—I'm pedaling as fast as I can," printed on it.

"It's for the back of your car," Ronny explained.

"It's lovely," my mother said faintly. "Thank you so much, Ronny."

We sat around for a while, and then Ronny went home, and my mother said now was a good time to begin indexing my Christmas cards in Aunt Clara's box.

"She may drop in, and I'd like you to be able to show

her how much you appreciate her gift," she said. "Besides, think how convenient it will be next Christmas, when you make out your list, to be able to tell at a glance who sent you cards this year."

We had a little discussion about this, but my mother started to get all upset and talk about the spirit of Christmas and putting ourselves out for other people, so I said I would do it.

First, though, I called Susie, and Pat called me, and I tried on my new silk blouse, and Judy called me, and Ronny came over again to play his album of Elvis Presley singing Christmas carols, and my mother made us turn it off, and Ronny went home, and then I indexed the cards.

It took forever; but by the time I got to the end, I had the satisfied feeling that comes when you've done something useless but that your mother has developed a thing about.

The last card at the bottom of the pile was just beautiful. I guess I had missed it before, in all the excitement. It was made of red satin with gold lettering. "Season's Greetings," it said, "from A. Bledsoe Smith."

"Who is he?" I asked my mother.

She studied the card. "Heavens, how should I know?" she asked. "It's a lovely card. Very expensive. Don't you recognize the name?"

"No," I said. "I can't imagine. I don't know anyone in school by that name. Could he be a relative?"

"No," she said. "Look at the envelope. Where was it postmarked?"

"Coulter's Falls, Minnesota," I said. We looked at each other.

"Are you sure it's not for someone else?" she asked.

"Remember when we got Mrs. Hale's electric bill by mistake and paid it?"

But the envelope was addressed to Miss Alicia Morrison, Elm Street, Carver, Connecticut. The handwriting was awful, but that's what it said.

"Well, it must be some boy you met at a dance or something and forgot," my mother said.

"I never in my life met anyone from Minnesota," I said. "Except my biology teacher, and he's from Wisconsin. And his name is Johnson."

We worried about it for a while—at least, my mother worried—and kept saying how expensive the card was and what a shame I hadn't sent one to him, whoever he was. Finally, we gave the whole thing up, and I wrote, "Smith, A. Bledsoe," on an index card and put it in the file and closed the box.

On New Year's Day we took down the tree, and I packed the box away with the Christmas ornaments in the basement, so naturally we didn't find it again until this past Christmas Eve, long after I had mailed my cards. This shows what a practical, useful gift it was.

This past Christmas Eve was ghastly, anyway. We had trouble setting up the tree, and some of our nicest ornaments were broken, and when we went to the midnight services, we saw all the families sitting together and felt lonely and left out, with just the two of us. My mother was wearing her blue-velvet hat and crying. I felt like crying myself. Ronny hadn't called me for three days because of a fight we had about Latin declensions, which ended with his calling me stupid. By the time we got home, my mother and I were too depressed to make eggnog and put carols on the record player, two sacred Christmas Eve traditions at our house. We just slumped on the sofa and glared at the tree, which was sort of leaning to one side and molting. Even the unopened presents piled around it looked uninteresting—mostly that flat shape meaning handkerchiefs or gloves.

"I think next year we should plan to go away during the holidays," my mother said.

"Go away where?" I asked.

"I don't know," my mother said.

We sat there awhile longer, listening to the pine needles drop to the carpet.

"Some more cards came for you this afternoon," my mother said. "They're on the coffee table. Why don't you open them?"

One was from my Girl Scout troop leader when I was twelve years old, and one was from my minister, and one was from a beauty parlor where I once had a permanent. Very heart-warming. But then there was a big, square one, all sequins and glitter and velvet holly sprigs.

"Season's Greetings from A. Bledsoe Smith," it said, and I began to cry. Isn't that crazy? My mother asked me what on earth was the matter.

"It's from that old A. B-Bledsoe S-Smith!" I wailed.

Then we both started to giggle, and pretty soon we were laughing like a couple of maniacs. We finally calmed down, and we made eggnog; but every time we looked at each other while we were drinking it, we would break into giggles.

It was beginning to feel like Christmas, after all.

At two o'clock we decided to go to bed, but just as I was walking through the hall, the phone rang. My mother gave a little scream. My mother thinks that if the phone rings after eight o'clock at night, it is because someone has been run over by a truck and taken to the emergency ward, where he is sinking fast.

"Hello?" I said.

There was a lot of crackling on the line, and the voices of operators arguing with each other about whose party should talk first, and plugs being pulled in and out of switchboards at distant places.

A man's voice came very faintly through the static.

"This is the Morrison residence," I said. "Who is this?"

All I could make out was that this man was calling from some airport someplace and would be over to see us tomorrow morning.

"Wonderful!" I shouted into the receiver. "Who did you say this was?"

There was more static, and the man's voice said a lot of things I could barely understand. One of the few things I did manage to hear clearly was the name Smith.

"Your party has hung up," the operator said. "Do you wish me to ring him back?"

"No," I said, and put down the receiver slowly. "It was A. Bledsoe Smith," I told my mother. "He's calling from someplace. He'll be over tomorrow."

"Oh?" my mother said.

"He can't wait to see me," I said. "It's been a long, long time, but he's never forgotten me."

"I hope he's tall enough for you," my mother said. "Is your crinoline clean?"

After I got into bed, I spent at least an hour running over all the dances and parties I had ever been to, trying to pick out the face of a mysterious boy who went away to Minnesota and never forgot me and sent expensive Christmas cards. It was no use.

We had just started to open our presents on Christmas morning when the doorbell rang.

"I'll go," my mother said.

139

I sat on the floor under the tree, and I had kicked off
my slippers to be more comfortable. I was wearing a laven-
der shirt and my green slacks, and didn't intend to put on
a dress until later.

"*In excelsis gloria!*" said a familiar voice.

I looked up. It was Ronny.

"That's Latin in case you didn't catch it," he explained
kindly.

"Where did you find that sweater?" I asked. "Trick or
treat?"

"Isn't it creepy?" he agreed, looking down at the stripes
and circles and pinwheels decorating it. "My mother gave
it to me. I think she's getting senile."

"It's a lovely gift," my mother said, and the doorbell rang
again.

This time I answered it.

"Is this the Morrison residence?" the man asked. He
was tall and handsome; he was everything I had imagined
A. Bledsoe Smith would be—except for one slight detail.
He was about forty years old.

"Are you—" I began. "I mean, you aren't—"

"Is Mrs. Morrison at home?" he asked. "I am—"

Just at this second, there was a gasp behind me, and my
mother rushed to the door, almost knocking me down.
She threw her arms around this man, and she shrieked,
"Artie! Artie! Is it really you?"

The two of them stood there hugging each other and
laughing and exclaiming and carrying on in a way that, if
I had done it, my mother would have given me lecture
number four on ladylike behavior with persons of the opposite sex.

Finally, they let go and came into the living room.

My mother introduced him. "It's Artie Smith!" she kept
babbling, as though she were simpleminded. "Why, we

haven't seen each other for seventeen years—since college! We even went steady for a while, didn't we, Artie?"

"All during our junior year," he said. "I read in the alumni magazine about your husband's death and sent you a Christmas card, but I never knew if it reached you."

"Your name—I never connected—" my mother said in bewilderment. "And Minnesota. How was I to dream you had moved there?"

"Well, Arthur Smith isn't a very impressive name for a lawyer," he explained. "When I began to handle some fairly big cases, I needed something to impress the judges. Bledsoe is my middle name."

And they went on and on about college and proms and the soda shop, and they giggled, and finally my mother went into her room, and after a while, when she came out, she was wearing her flannel slacks and—I could hardly believe my eyes!—my very best white cashmere sweater. *She* had borrowed *my* sweater! I was just about to say something when she told me that she and A. Bledsoe Smith were going to take a walk in the snow, and, when they came back, he was going to take us to dinner at the inn.

"Before you leave," I said coldly—I felt that this whole thing was getting a little out of hand—"may I ask, Mr. Smith, how come you sent those Christmas cards to *me*?"

"I didn't," said A. Bledsoe Smith. "I sent them to Mrs. Tricia Morrison. May I ask how come you opened them?"

"Think of your remembering my old nickname!" my mother cooed.

"Well, it looked like Miss Alicia Morrison," I said.

"I always had awful handwriting," said A. Bledsoe Smith, without a trace of remorse.

Then they went out—this man and my own mother, who had highhandedly taken possession not only of my

141

white cashmere sweater, but also of my mysterious suitor and my long-distance telephone call and my two expensive Christmas cards.

"Well!" I said.

"What's in that nutty-looking package?" Ronny asked, pointing. He was down on the floor, studying all our presents.

I sat down beside him, picked up the package he had pointed to, and then opened it in a daze. Something told me that things were starting this morning that would change every Christmas to come. Something told me that next time we went to midnight services on Christmas Eve, we would look like a family again. I hadn't decided yet whether I approved.

"What is it?" Ronny asked.

I lifted the cover. "It's from my aunt Clara," I said. "It's an earring box."

"It is not," Ronny said. "There is no such thing."

"It is too," I said. "See—it has all these little compartments that you're supposed to put a pair of earrings in. It holds up to fifty pairs of earrings, it says here on the tag."

"Cripes!" Ronny said.

"I don't have any earrings to put in it at all," I said listlessly.

"Yes, you do," Ronny said, and handed me a little package. Inside was the most beautiful pair of earrings I ever saw—all made of pearls and some kind of blue stone, and real dangly, like tassels.

"Oh, Ronny, they're gorgeous!" I said. "I bet my mother won't let me wear them."

"I bet she will," Ronny said. "I bet you one hundred dollars if you put them on and she sees them when she comes back, she won't say a word."

I put them on, and they felt as if they dangled to my

shoulders. They were absolutely beautiful. "I bet you one hundred dollars she'll make me take them right off," I said.

But you know what? When my mother and this A. Bledsoe Smith came home from their walk in the snow, my mother's face was all flushed, and her hair was blown by the wind, and she said to me, "Hello, darling. What in heaven's name are you wearing?"

"Ronny gave them to me," I said. "They're earrings."

"What a lovely gift!" my mother said.

So I owe Ronny one hundred dollars.

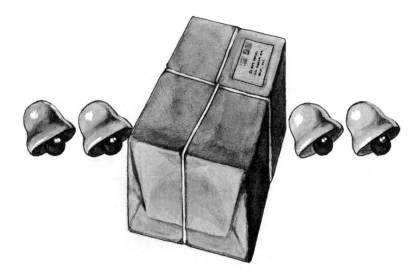

LAST DELIVERY
BEFORE CHRISTMAS

Ernest Buckler

My father had been dead two years, and that August my mother married again. She married Syd Weston. It was that circumstance which. . . . But you would have to understand quite thoroughly about Mother and Syd and me to have any of that following Christmas make sense.

For Mother's sake I tried not to let resentment of my stepfather show. But a child of ten doesn't have the technique for that kind of acting. *I* didn't, anyway. I remember how angry I used to get with my face sometimes. Other people's faces could keep a secret for them. But whenever I'd glimpse mine in any reflecting surface it seemed to be tattling everything that went on behind it.

I suppose I got that from my father, though with a crucial difference. His face used to be right out with everything too, but in an expansive, entirely unselfconscious way. I believe, if you'd asked him to describe his face, he'd have had to think a minute to know what it really looked like. (Where had that outward look gone, I wondered, the day they took me in to look at him, with the flower smell like a silence gone sickly in the parlor, and the yellower sections of the drawn-down blinds like the first hint of a mortality even in the green fields outside?)

He never turned things over in his mind as I did. I suppose I got that from Mother. I have that curse of sensing immediately the degree of discordance among any group I enter—with a sort of responsibility, as if the guilt for it were my own. Mother had that too.

That's why most of the time I tried to hide from her how Syd and I jarred. Syd's face hardly told on him at all. It just seemed to listen.

Syd was no stranger. His small, tidy farm was right next to ours. There wasn't even a fence along the line between us. I remember that when Father would mow

146

there first the swath would go across the line and back, crooked as a ram's horn, but when Syd made the first cut his swath would be straight as a die, just inside the line on his part.

The only time I had ever seen Syd's face give him away was the day of my father's funeral. Heartbroken though I was that day, I studied everyone's face, as any child will, to see how they were feeling and to see what kind of look each of them was giving me. A simulated grief sat on the other faces like a kind of demureness, but Syd's face had such a look it startled me right out of myself. It had a sort of desperate, waking-in-a-strange-place look, especially when he glanced at Mother.

He would never come into our house after that. But how many times, it seemed by accident, he would be working alongside the road when I went by and ask me how we were making out. And it got so I went over to his place quite a bit. He would let me take the reins of the team until we came to a ditch or had to cross the main road, and he let me pick out small rocks to chink the well with, in a way that made me feel as if I were grown-up and doing a man's work. I remember how I'd spit sideways when both my hands were busy, the way men do.

I never felt any constraint with him then—unless some of the other kids came by; then I'd make some excuse to leave immediately. Because, among ourselves, we called him "old man Weston." Not because he was old or cranky, but because he lived alone. And no one is as cruelly ostracized by kids as someone a little different.

I remember one day I said to him, "Syd, why didn't you ever get married?" It used to be a gig of mine to try to startle people with odd questions like that. But Syd's face didn't alter a bit.

"Well now, I don't know," he said.

147

"Y'know, Syd," I said, "you look real good when you're dressed up and Mum said you used to be the best dancer she ever danced with!"

"Did she now!" he said. His face didn't change then either, but he brushed away the shavings from the auger hole he was boring with a sudden little movement that reminded me somehow of the way a dust devil will catch at a neat windrow of hay and disarrange it.

He never talked about Mother directly. But occasionally when I would do or say something that I couldn't see was any way different from the way anyone else would do or say it, he would murmur, "Ain't that Laura for you!" Laura was my mother.

I knew, of course, that Syd had gone with Mother when they were both young from hearing the women joke with her about it sometimes. "Do you mind how we used to cross out Syd Weston's name with yours in school and they'd both come out 'marriage'?" or "Is it true that Syd was hangin' off till he had a hundred dollars in the bank?"

And I knew how Jess Matthews (that was my father) had come here to Westfield with a lumbering crew and married her within a month. It was a sort of local legend how that night at the pie social when he did the tricks (he could do tricks that *no* one could see through) he got Mother to come up and hold out her left hand and, after exhibiting his own empty palms and rolling up his sleeves, made a quick magician's gesture in the air and before she knew it there was an engagement ring on her finger, and she standing there looking as if she didn't know whether she wanted to laugh or cry.

Father was always laughing, or ready to laugh. He'd pay the fiddler as much as five dollars to play an extra hour at the Friday-night dances in the schoolhouse, and there was always a bunch of kids hanging around him.

He could turn out to have completely forgotten something he'd promised you, something you'd counted on for days, and then with just some conspiratorial little nudge or wink become as infallible as ever and make you feel as big and wonderful as he was.

I mentioned that pie-social affair to Mother one time. "Was Syd there that night?" I asked.

"No," she said. "He had to haul in grain. He said, 'It looks like rain, and if that load of oats gets wet again tonight, it won't be good for anything.'"

That'd be Syd all right. And then I thought, Wasn't it funny that anyone would recall the words—the exact words —someone else had said about a little thing like that so long ago?

Syd never came inside our house again until that August evening. He'd give us a load of wood now and then, but he'd haul it into the dooryard some afternoon Mother was away. And she'd send *me* to thank him and try to make him take pay for it. And whenever Mother would bring out a plate of cake and a jug of lemonade to the men in the afternoon, Syd always seemed to be off in a corner someplace, clipping around a rock (every haying season Father planned to blast the big rocks in the field that fall, but somehow he never got it done) with the hand scythe.

I can still remember that August evening. I remember how peculiarly still it was. I had gone to bed before dark, so I could run off all by myself, like a reel in my head, the excitement of going away. Mother had finally made up her mind.

From my bed by the window I could see Syd sitting on the front doorstep of his small house. To a child the idea of oneself going away makes sober, rooted people seem almost incredible, unbelievably stupid. You feel that somehow someone should make them *understand*.

149

Ernest Buckler

The stillness didn't bother me, but I know now the kind of stillness it was for the older ones. It was one of those nights of drought when the slamming of a screen door or the tapping of a neighbor's hammer sounds astonishingly near. And yet everything else seems untouchably far away. There is only the fitful pulse of the blind against the screen where you sit, hearing only your mind not-think.

I saw Mother go outside. She walked along the edge of the flower bed, picking off a wilted nasturtium leaf here and there or straightening the sticks beside the rosebushes. But she did these things inertly, as you do things on a day you are trying to whittle away with movement—a day when it seems as if each time you look at the clock more time must have passed than the clock has counted.

I knew Mother wasn't happy, like me, about going away. But what could she do? A farm can go on for a few years without a man's steady care, but what can a woman do when the ditches in the low parts grass over and fill in, and the shingles blow up on the very top of the barn roof, and the time comes when all the fence wire is rusted too brittle even to splice? Even if she could pay to have these things fixed, what about the night when the gale blows the big shed doors open or the day the cow is choking on an apple and no one within sound of your call?

It was coming dusk when I saw Alf Steele walking up the road. He stopped for a minute opposite Syd's. Their voices came to me clear as voices over water.

"Ain't ya comin' to school meetin', Syd?" Alf called.

"I guess not," Syd answered. "Not tonight."

"No? Well. . . ." And then, just before resuming his pace, Alf added, "Did ya know Laura's goin' away? Anyhow, that's the talk."

"Goin' away?" Syd said. "No. Where?"

150

"They say her brother Frank's got her a job in the city. Montreal, ain't it, Frank is?"

Syd came to his feet so quickly I thought he was going out to the road to question Alf further. But he didn't. He turned abruptly and went inside the house.

It couldn't have been more than fifteen minutes later that I heard our screen door open and close.

"Why, Syd!" Mother exclaimed. The heat hole over the kitchen stove was right beside my bed, and I could catch everything that was said below.

"I can't set down," Syd blurted out. "I just came over to. . . ."

I knew he did sit down, though. In my mind I could picture him snapping the crown of his cap to the peak and unsnapping it. And I could see Mother taking off her apron and smoothing out the wrinkles in her skirt. I could see her place a smile on her face consciously. It wouldn't be a false smile, but it wouldn't hide her feelings half as thoroughly as she believed.

"Laura," Syd said—and the words came out propulsively, as if they were a stoppage in his throat—"you ain't goin' away, are you?"

I could see the precarious smile drop off Mother's face. "I don't know, Syd," she said. Her voice sounded freer, now that her thought and her speech need not keep to separate channels. "I guess so. I don't know what to do. I can't seem to think. Frank wants me to go out there with him. I wouldn't like the city, I know, but things here have got to the point where. . . ." She would be sitting there ironing one arm with the palm of her other hand.

There was quite a long silence. And then I heard Syd say, "Don't, Laura . . . don't. . . ." I knew what had happened. I always hated to see Mother cry. She'd draw in a deep breath and hold it hard, as if against the muscles of her face. But then the muscles would begin to give way, one group after another. And her mouth would look as if it hurt her, physically.

"I guess I'm making a fool of myself," Mother said, all at once contrite. "Do you remember what you used to say, 'I never saw how crying over anything ever helped'?"

I heard a chair scrape then. Syd would be standing there, clumsy with the thought of his hand lying on her shoulder and equally clumsy with the thought of taking it away, because it seemed to help her, touched for a moment by that curious glow you feel when someone puts a particular memory of you into words, when you had feared that nothing more than a general memory of you might exist in anyone anywhere.

"Laura," he said suddenly, "*don't* go 'way. Why couldn't you and me . . . ?" I think she looked up, surprised and not surprised. And then he spoke almost with savagery. "I ain't the old"—he couldn't seem to find the word which should come next—"people think I am. I got feelin's too."

I had a moment of consternation. It sounded as if Syd hated the way he was. It had never occurred to me that all people in any way strange might have to go on being that way because other people kept expecting it of them.

And then I covered my head with the bedclothes not to hear any more. I knew we would not be going away now.

But even that was crowded out of my mind. I had only one bitter, burning thought. You needn't be openly rebellious against a usurper, but if you observed forever one little obstinacy known only to yourself, your original loyalty would still be intact. For Mother's sake I wouldn't make any fuss. But I would go right on calling him Syd. I would never, *never* call him Dad.

I think that at the beginning Mother didn't really worry at all about my keeping Syd at arm's length. It was to be expected. But in a few weeks, when the situation hadn't changed, a constraint fell over all of us. This constraint was not continuous, of course; three people cannot live together in the country without being unreservedly fused most of the time by little excitements, little catastrophes, and the news brought in by one or the other from outside. But I had the child's talent for that most punishing rebuke: of withdrawing a little, as if behind an invisible boundary, just when the other has begun to think your estrangement must have been something he imagined.

Syd would show me how to mow, placing my hands just so on the scythe and I trying to hold them right there; then, following my swath, he'd say, "That's right, that's right, you got the hang of it," and I'd say, "I guess you can finish it," and go hang up the scythe in the crotch of a tree. Or we might be preparing to go raspberrying in the back burntland, searching about for the water jug, gathering the tins, checking in the lunch basket to see if the salt and pepper for the eggs hadn't been forgotten, and I'd turn to Mother and say, "Is *he* going to stay all day with us?"

It was then that Mother's face would get that awful look: resignation, but resignation worse for never being safe from a hope perpetually renewed and as perpetually struck down. She would sometimes pass her hand over her forehead vaguely as if there were some possible kind of motion that would wipe this film over things away. And for a while after that it would seem as if everything Syd and I said (or didn't say) to each other sounded sort of loud.

153

Ernest Buckler

The situation was never openly admitted, and at first
Mother tried to overcome it. If I let slip something spon-
taneous like, "I'd like to see Syd on that mowin' machine
o' Reg's. I bet he could mow that field in two hours!" she'd
seize upon my remark and repeat it to him ever so casually.
Or if Syd were to say, "Why, that kid can sow grass seed
as good as a man—better'n *some* men!" she'd repeat that to
me. But her casualness was so transparent (each of us
knew what the situation was) that her ruses turned out
to be only embarrassing. And after a little she gave them
up.

Otherwise, things certainly went smoother with us than
they had ever done when Father was alive. There was always dry wood in the shed, the water pails were always
full, the clothesline was now spliced so strong it never let
Mother's clean sheets down into the mud, and . . . well,
that precarious bridge from one day to the next seemed
to be completely shored up.

But how could a child love anyone for that kind of
thing? How could that kind of thoughtfulness take the
place of the knack Father had of immediately winning you
over to his way of seeing that serious concern over *any-*
thing belonged way down below fun?

It was queer about that, though. Once Mother lost the
new scissors she'd spent the last cent in her purse for.
"Now where could I have laid them?" she said, frowning
with worry. "Did you have 'em openin' the flour bag?"
Father asked. "No." "Didn't have 'em out clippin flowers?"
"No, I had the little scissors out there." He thought. "Sure
you didn't have 'em cuttin' up citron for a pound cake?"
She had laughed so we'd had to be stern with her to keep
her from hysterics. But the minute her laughter had subsided her face looked as worried as before. Now when she

154

laughed with Syd about anything—though less often and not half as hysterically—an echo of the laughter would stay on in her eyes long after the laughter itself was done.

If only half-consciously, I resented that. I would think: if he'd ever once do something that wasn't so darned sensible, so darned predictable.

It was only when I would actually surprise myself in a moment of accepting Syd wholeheartedly that I was deliberately cruel to him.

I remember one day I was watching him make a birdhouse for me, completely engrossed in the expert way his large hands could manage the miniature splices. I was fingering absently a little gadget that hung from the buttonhole of my jacket. It was a tiny cube of wood, whittled so that only a sphere remained inside its open-faced cage.

He looked up. "Ronnie," he said, "one o' them edges there is way longer than the others. Let me square her up for you."

I bridled. "Naw," I said, "don't bother. That's all right."

"It won't take but a minute," he said. "Let's see it."

I moved off. "Naw, that's all right," I said. "My father made me that."

He didn't say a word.

Another day a cattle buyer was looking at the oxen. I felt just like a third man with him and Syd. Syd never said anything like, "Now keep friggin' with that sprayer till ya break it!" or "Look outa the man's way there," the way other men (even Father) did, to cut down kids in the barn.

"You oughta seen the rock that team hauled off last week!" I said.

The buyer grinned at me. "That's quite a boy you got there, Mr. Weston," he said, in a hearty salesman's voice.

155

"I guess he's gonna be as good a judge o' cattle as his old man, eh?"

"He's not my old man," I said. "My father is dead."

I was glad Mother didn't see Syd's face then. Come to think of it, perhaps it used to give him away more often than I've made it sound.

I think the fortnight before Christmas must have been the worst of all for Mother. She was very happy because we had more money for the mail order that year than ever before, and I knew she kept waiting for me to study the catalogue, so that she could glimpse which page I kept it open at longest. But I acted as if Christmas didn't matter to me in the least. Other years I used to nag and nag at her to get the order off early. But that year it was she herself who had to say, "My soul, this is the fifteenth. We better get that order off this very night or it'll be too late."

The night when we used to clear off the dining-room table and get out all the writing paraphernalia, pretending we were ordering each other's gifts from one page in the catalogue, while a finger was holding it open, secretly, to another; with her putting down the things for me and then folding the order sheet over her writing until I had put her gifts below; and making a solemn promise that when she added up the total she wouldn't even glance at anything but the figures—that night used to be almost as exciting as Christmas itself.

But that year I let her sit at the table alone. It gave me an almost sickening pang to see her there, taking as long as ever to select those things for me which would be useful but still have something of the "present" quality about them, and sobered (but so unprotestingly) by my withholding of connivance in the spirit of the occasion thus made so desolate for her to support alone. But I couldn't help it. I didn't even pretend to glance at the numbers of the pages she was copying from.

Once she said, so extra casually I knew it had come on her tongue and then faltered a good many times before she could speak it, "Would you like to put something down for your father?" Syd was outside.

I knew it would have delighted her beyond anything if I'd answered something like, "Yeah. What could I get him? Something that would really surprise him!" But what I said was, "No, I guess not. It'd be kinda foolish gettin' him something with his own money."

I didn't put anything down for him or, because it would be paid for with his money, for her either. Syd himself had never once inquired what I wanted. If he had, I was prepared to say, "Oh, anything. I don't care," with deliberate indifference. But just the same, I almost hated him for not asking.

Syd took the letter to the post office the next morning. Any letter that needed a money order fixed up for enclosure Mother usually took. But he offered specially almost insisted, to take this one. For a moment I wondered if he wanted to look at the sheet to see if there was anything on it for him (and for a moment I had another pang: to think of this little curiosity being rewarded by the sight of nothing more exciting than a work shirt). But then I knew that spying wasn't like Syd. This would be just like any other letter to him, I thought.

Times before, the day the Christmas order had finally gone off had been one of the wonderful ones. It had seemed as if we'd set in motion some benevolent mechanism that would be busy contriving something splendid for us all through the following days, even when we were not thinking about it. But that morning this mood of indifference I had chosen spoiled everything.

About ten o'clock, Mother's hand froze suddenly on the pump handle. "Oh, dear!" she said. "I forgot to put down the tissue paper and seals. Now isn't that . . . ?"

She looked at me appealingly. I thought, If I'd only helped her (though the bitter regret which the *only* implied was disowned almost as soon as I recognized it). *I* wouldn't have forgotten. But I didn't say a word. And after that, Mother suddenly gave up trying to encourage my Christmas spirit.

It is curious how a child will prolong a sort of sulkiness that has started as whim until it hardens into obstinacy, resisting every effort to dislodge him from it, and how the most dismaying thing of all is when the others at last take his mood at its face value and leave him entirely alone.

I was, however, to know a dismay even worse before the next week was out.

Christmas was on Saturday of that week, and the order should come on the Tuesday or Wednesday before. But it didn't come Tuesday—or Wednesday. And when I went to the post office on Thursday, certain that it would be there (and thankful by this time that the excitement of the package arriving could save my face by seeming to sweep me out of my mood, rather than my having to abandon it of my own free will), the package was not there either. There was just a card, saying it had gone to the station. Whenever you have deliberately chosen to be perverse, it seems that everything else is quick to fall into line.

"Now what did they send it by express for?" Mother said. "I can't think of anything heavy in it."

"It's cheaper that way," Syd said.

"I know," Mother said. "But Christmas time . . . when everyone's in such a rush. . . . ."

"We can give the card to Cliff tomorrow," Syd said—Cliff was the mailman—"and he'll go to the station and get it for us."

"Why, yes," Mother said. "I never thought of that. Cliff'll get it. He's a good soul."

I was so relieved I nearly cried.

That night the snow came. When Syd came in from his late trip to the barn he stood in the porch almost solid white, with his arms angled out from his sides for someone to brush him off with the broom. "Why, Syd!" Mother cried, "Is it snowing? Like *that?*" And after I'd gone up to bed I kept my lamp lit for a little while to watch the great flakes float and eddy down past the window pane, like an infinite fragmentation of some beautiful white healing silence. Snow for Christmas.

But with it, while I slept, the wind came.

And when I looked out the window in the morning the whole world seemed buried in a great sea of snow: huge, billowing, porpoise-backed waves of it, caught up around the corners of the buildings into long breaker tips that reached almost to the eaves. I saw Syd starting to shovel a tunnel to the barn. He didn't bend, but reached, at the drift before him. Here and there a spot of road would show bare as your hand in a trough of the waves, but on either side of the spot you couldn't even guess where the road went. I looked again at Syd's tunnel. He had scraped it right down to the grass, but I saw that already the wind had sifted enough snow back into it that a deep track could be made.

I knew that the men would not break out the roads until the wind had died down completely. Not till afternoon, anyway. I knew the mail would not go today. And this was the last day before Christmas. And so the order would never get here for Christmas at all.

I thought, for a second, how I had almost believed in my indifference to Christmas a couple of weeks ago. How could that have been possible? Was this storm, like the order going to the station, some sort of punishment? Perhaps the mere focusing of memory on it tends to exaggerate a past despair. But it seems to me that those moments when I stood there at the window, realizing for the first time that the unthinkable *could* happen, may well have been the bleakest of my whole life.

Mother tried her best to console me. She said we had the tree, anyway (Syd had got that a couple of days ago, an absolutely perfect one), and we had lots of candy and nuts, and, well, the things would be only a little late. I could hardly keep from shouting when I answered, "What good are things *after* Christmas?" Especially with no tissue paper to wrap them in, and the time already past before which they must not be opened. It would be just like an order you'd sent in the summertime.

Syd didn't say a word. He didn't seem to be disturbed at all. And later in the morning, when I stood in the porch door, praying that by some last-minute miracle I'd see the ox teams come breaking the roads and the mailman's horse behind them (though the wind was blowing stronger now rather than less), I heard Mother say to him almost frantically, "Syd, what could we fix up for Ronnie? We've just got to have something for him."

He said, "I don't know. What could we fix up for him?" But he didn't sound really concerned. In the next breath he asked her if she could get dinner early. I couldn't see

160

what difference it made when we ate, or if we ate at all, with the whole long, empty day ahead.

After an early dinner, we started to trim the tree. Mother and I. Syd got out his rifle and took it apart to clean it.

I helped Mother as conscientiously as I had ever done, because I was too desolate even to be sullen. But I worked with that awful docility with which you put on your best clothes as carefully as ever though the occasion is a farewell at the train, maybe for the last time. And then a shaft of how it might have been—trimming the tree on this cloistering day (the wind was shriller now), with the contents of the order hidden no more secretly than beneath the sofa and, because of that, my pledge not to look all the more torturingly sweet—would pierce me right to the bone.

About one o'clock, Syd came into the parlor. "I think I'll take a scout around with the gun," he said. So that's why he'd wanted an early dinner.

"Syd," Mother exclaimed, "you're not going hunting, a day like this?"

"It's a good day for huntin'," he said. "The wind'd be just about right in the spruce, and the snowshoein' ain't bad."

In one direction from our house was the road to town and in the other, across some narrow fields, was the dense woods. Twenty solid miles of it.

"Well . . . " Mother said resignedly. "But now you watch out a tree doesn't fall on you or something."

I was so shocked that Syd could leave us alone on this day that I didn't even resent it. I just watched him go across the field, lost in and then appearing out of the spasmodic gusts of wind-driven snow as if he were evaporating and then solidifying again.

We didn't pay much attention to the storm until we had finished working on the tree. In the morning the wind had blown hard, but unconcernedly. Now it was getting rough. Not vicious yet, but rough.

"I wonder if he took his compass," Mother said suddenly. She went to the pantry. The compass was still hanging on its nail. I knew you couldn't lose Syd if you tried, but just the same I was half-annoyed at her for checking up on the compass. It would have been more comfortable not to have known he didn't have it.

About three o'clock the wind grew really vicious, like an animal become ravening with the taste of its own violence. The air looked like one of those blizzards that sheep on an old calendar are seen huddling against. The trees bent and writhed constantly, and the wind howled at the corners of the house as it sucked itself wildly across the fields.

And now, as if out of some place wrenched open by the wind, the cold came, depositing its sharp knives on the panes.

As the afternoon wore on, the uneasiness in both of us grew to active worry. But neither of us mentioned it. Partly as if by not naming it you could achieve protection, however flimsy, from the thing you feared, and partly because it had become so difficult for us to discuss Syd at all, let alone a mutual concern for him.

We tried to fake an interest in small tasks. But the instant there'd be a slight lull in the storm, one or the other would immediately say, "I believe it's lettin' up," or "Of course, inside it always looks worse than it is." The next instant a redoubled clap of wind would make the chimney gasp as if the very breath of the house were being sucked outside to be spun about, captured, and lost forever, and our automatic glances at each other would seem to collide with almost physical effect—as glances do when smoke is discovered curling out from some place where no smoke should be.

And then we began one at a time to make excuses, peering out the frosted window toward the woods. The Christmas tree was like a mockery. It was like the guest from another way of life who happens to be staying with you when some private trouble strikes, so that you are denied even a natural as-with-neighbors reaction to it, because of appearance's sake.

It got so the only things of any reality in the whole house seemed to be Syd's unspoken name and the tick of the clock. And it was odd the situations my mind chose to recall him in: always one something like his maybe looking at the order sheet and seeing nothing for him there but the work shirt.

About four, Mother got supper. "Syd'll be hungry," she said, "after the early dinner and tramping in the woods." But I knew that was only an excuse. I knew she had the foolish idea that supper ready would somehow beckon him home.

But supper was ready and then growing cold on the back of the stove, and still he hadn't come. And then supper *waiting* made the whole thing more clamorous than ever. It was early, but already there was a hint of darkness coming. As if the wind had broken into the hold of night too, and let dusk loose beforehand.

Just then the clock struck the half hour. Suddenly Mother leaped up. "He should be home now," she said. "I'm going down to Alf's and see if he thinks we ought to. . . ."

I leaped up too. I felt an inexpressible relief, now that this intolerable pretense of casualness was over.

"I'm goin' with you," I said. I expected her to oppose that, but she didn't.

163

"Well . . . all right," she said.

I got my heavy clothes on first and went in to look out the parlor window once more—openly, avidly now. There was nothing but that marching blur and the mourning trees. When she was ready she came in too.

"See any sign of him?" she said.

"No," I said. She looked as if the muscles of her face were starting to break up.

We were just turning from the window when all at once she put her hand on my arm. "Hark!" she said. "Wasn't that the back door?"

We both rushed to the kitchen. And there he was, standing by the door, the snow so driven into his clothes, and his eyebrows and mustache so encrusted with it, that he was hardly recognizable.

"Syd," Mother cried, "oh Syd. . . ." She ran and put her arms about him and her face against his shoulder, snow and all.

"What's the trouble?" Syd said, startled. "What's wrong?" It had never occurred to him that we'd be worried on his account. He thought something dreadful must have happened to *us*.

"You," Mother cried. "You . . . out in this. We've been almost crazy. Where have you been?" Her questions tumbled over each other before he could get out a single word. "Where did you come from? We didn't see you. We've been watching the woods all afternoon, haven't we, Ronnie? Where's your gun? Were you lost?"

"I didn't come by the woods," Syd said. "I came by the road."

"The road? Here, let me shake that jumper off in the woodbox. You'll get your death." (I ran into the pantry for a knife to scrape the icicles off.) "Where's your gun?"

Syd sort of grinned. "In the barn," he said. The barn was way down from the house, in the opposite direction from the woods.

"The *barn?*"

Syd didn't answer. He opened the door and reached back into the porch. I thought he was reaching for the old broom.

When he straightened up, I couldn't believe my eyes. Everyone knows one miracle in his life, and this was mine. For in his hand he carried the Christmas order!

"Syd!" Mother cried. "You've been to town! You lugged that order all the way home!" Then, for a second, plain curiosity displaced her agitation. "Is that *our* order?" she said. "Look at the size of it, and the shape of it. I don't remember. . . ." It was a huge package, obviously containing some long, almost unwrappable object at the bottom. No wonder it had gone to the station.

I couldn't say a word. I was inundated by the soft glow of danger past, the Christmas order was right here in the house, the tree had suddenly become an intimate again, and now the wind and the cold and the dark were not enemies anymore, just things that could be let go their way, their violence merely heightening the sense of our own containment.

But it was not so much any of that as something else. It was as if I were seeing in Syd a different man. It wasn't that he had walked six miles to town and back on a day like this to get the order. It was that he had wanted to *surprise* us. It was that he had gone to all that maneuver of pretended indifference, of cleaning his gun, of actually going into the woods while we watched, and then cutting back across the field, leaving his gun in the barn, and skirting the pasture till he struck the road to town. It was that, for this effect of surprise, he had done something that had so little common sense about it, that was so crazy, it was almost childish. . . .

And when he fished way down inside the very last layer of heavy clothing and said, "Didn't you mention somethin' about forgettin' to order the tissue paper and seals," and I knew he had got even them, at some store in town . . . well, I had still another thing to bless them for: for not remarking on my speechlessness, for making their own voices loud enough to cover up the other sound I couldn't help—crying.

Syd brushed the snow from the package and took it into the dining room to unwrap, while Mother was taking up the supper. When she went down the cellar for the creamer he came to the dining-room door and beckoned to me. I went in and he closed the door.

He had put all the parcels under the couch except one. It was on the dining-room table. A bright enameled case, with the top up and, inside, what I thought must surely be the most gorgeous comb, brush, and mirror set anyone had ever seen.

I gasped. He must have added that at the post office, I thought, the morning he took the order over. He (Syd!) must have asked the postmistress for her catalogue. I almost cried again: to think of what an effort that must have been for him, and of him trying to squeeze the article number and description in the tiny spaces provided, with that big handwriting of his that always looked as if it came so hard. I'd never touched anything with such reverence as the heavy mirror I picked up and then laid back again into its pleated satin socket.

"Think we could wrap it up kinda nice?" Syd said, almost sheepishly.

"Now?" I said. "Right now?"

"Might as well," he said. "Case she goes snoopin'."

It did look nice when we were done. I wouldn't have believed Syd could turn the corners of the flimsy tissue paper so deftly and hold them so perfectly in line while I put on the very biggest seals in the whole package. We hid it in the sideboard drawer, beneath the tablecloth.

Mother looked up when we came into the kitchen. Her face had that odd blend of caution and hope. "Now what are you two up to?" she said.

"Ask him," I said, grinning. "Ask Dad."

Maybe I only seem to remember that a swift, locking glance passed between them before they dropped their eyes. But I do know that Mother's face had the most indescribable look on it. As if something had divided her between such perfect joy and such fear that such perfect joy could not last.

But the next morning, with the wind composed and penitent again, and in the lamplight before dawn, when I saw the package beneath the tree that *no* one could wrap —the bright, gleaming, new twenty-two rifle that Syd must have added also at the post office—then, I think, she knew it would last.

"D'ya like it?" Syd said shyly. He didn't touch the twenty-two himself, but he kept standing near it all the time.

"*Like* it?" I said.

"But, Syd," Mother said, "do you think he's old enough for a gun?"

"Oh, Mother!" I cried.

"Now, stop worryin'!" Syd chided her. "There ain't nothin' about a gun, if anyone's careful."

She still didn't look too happy about it. But I think that, in a funny way, this was the most rewarding thing for her of all—that Syd and I were taking sides against her. With

167

that peculiar sense of omniscience that seems to come only with intense happiness, I thought (as a child thinks such things, recognizing the essence only of words that would express them), Now, at last, with the man and the boy disputing with the woman the wisdom of a gun for the boy, we are a family.

And I knew that, though I had no real gift for either of them, somehow I managed to give them a present better than any to be found in the catalogue.

And I knew too, if I could see it, wherever it was, my father's face would be right in on this with us; if I could hear him, he would be saying, "Now, y'see? What did I tell you about your frettin'? Everything always turns out right."

THE THEFT
OF THE ROYAL RUBY

Agatha Christie

"**I** regret exceedingly . . ." said M. Hercule Poirot.
He was interrupted. Not rudely interrupted. The interruption was suave, dexterous, persuasive rather than contradictory.

"Please don't refuse offhand, Monsieur Poirot. There are grave issues of state. Your cooperation will be appreciated in the highest quarters."

"You are too kind"—Hercule Poirot waved a hand—"but I really cannot undertake to do as you ask. At this season of the year. . . ."

Again Mr. Jesmond interrupted. "Christmas time," he said persuasively. "An old-fashioned Christmas in the English countryside."

Hercule Poirot shivered. The thought of the English countryside at this season of the year did not attract him.

"A good old-fashioned Christmas!" Mr. Jesmond stressed it.

"Me—I am not an Englishman," said Hercule Poirot. "In my country, Christmas, it is for the children. The New Year, that is what we celebrate."

"Ah," said Mr. Jesmond, "but Christmas in England is a great institution, and I assure you at Kings Lacey you would see it at its best. It's a wonderful old house, you know. Why, one wing of it dates from the fourteenth century."

Again Poirot shivered. The thought of a fourteenth-century English manor house filled him with apprehension. He had suffered too often in the historic country houses of England. He looked around appreciatively at his comfortable modern flat with its radiators and the latest patent devices for excluding any kind of draft.

"In the winter," he said firmly, "I do not leave London."

"I don't think you quite appreciate, Monsieur Poirot,

what a very serious matter this is." Mr. Jesmond glanced at his companion and then back at Poirot.

Poirot's second visitor had up to now said nothing but a polite and formal "How do you do." He sat now, gazing down at his well-polished shoes, with an air of the utmost dejection on his coffee-colored face. He was a young man, not more than twenty-three, and he was clearly in a state of complete misery.

"Yes, yes," said Hercule Poirot. "Of course the matter is serious. I do appreciate that. His Highness has my heartfelt sympathy."

"The position is one of the utmost delicacy," said Mr. Jesmond.

Poirot transferred his gaze from the young man to his older companion. If one wanted to sum up Mr. Jesmond in a word, the word would have been *discretion*. Everything about Mr. Jesmond was discreet. His well-cut but inconspicuous clothes, his agreeable, well-bred voice, which rarely soared out of an agreeable monotone, his light-brown hair just thinning a little at the temples, his pale, serious face. It seemed to Hercule Poirot that he had known not one Mr. Jesmond but a dozen Mr. Jesmonds in his time, all using sooner or later the same phrase—"a position of the utmost delicacy."

"The police," said Hercule Poirot, "can be very discreet, you know."

Mr. Jesmond shook his head firmly. "Not the police," he said. "To recover the—er—what we want to recover will almost inevitably involve taking proceedings in the law courts, and we know so little. We *suspect*, but we do not *know*."

"You have my sympathy," said Hercule Poirot again. If he imagined that his sympathy was going to mean anything to his two visitors, he was wrong. They did not want sympathy; they wanted practical help. Mr. Jesmond began once more to talk about the delights of an English Christmas.

"It's dying out, you know," he said, "the real old-fashioned type of Christmas. People spend it at hotels nowadays. But an English Christmas with all the family gathered around, the children and their stockings, the Christmas tree, the turkey and plum pudding, the crackers. The snowman outside the window. . . ."

In the interests of exactitude, Hercule Poirot intervened. "To make a snowman one has to have the snow," he remarked severely. "And one cannot have snow to order, even for an English Christmas."

"I was talking to a friend of mine in the meteorological office only today," said Mr. Jesmond, "and he tells me that it is highly probable there *will* be snow this Christmas."

It was the wrong thing to have said. Hercule Poirot shuddered more forcefully than ever. "Snow in the country!" he said. "That would be still more abominable. A large, cold, stone manor house."

"Not at all," said Mr. Jesmond. "Things have changed in the last ten years or so. Oil-fired central heating."

"They have oil-fired central heating at Kings Lacey?" asked Poirot. For the first time he seemed to waver.

Mr. Jesmond seized his opportunity. "Yes, indeed," he said, "and a splendid hot-water system. Radiators in every bedroom. I assure you, my dear Monsieur Poirot, Kings Lacey is comfort itself in the wintertime. You might even find the house *too* warm."

"That is most unlikely," said Hercule Poirot.

With practiced dexterity Mr. Jesmond shifted his ground a little. "You can appreciate the terrible dilemma we are in," he said, in a confidential manner.

Hercule Poirot nodded. The problem was, indeed, not a happy one. A young potentate-to-be, the only son of the ruler of a rich and important state had arrived in London a few weeks ago. His country had been passing through a period of restlessness and discontent. Though loyal to the father whose way of life had remained persistently Eastern, popular opinion was somewhat dubious of the younger generation. His follies had been Western ones and as such looked upon with disapproval.

Recently, however, his betrothal had been announced. He was to marry a cousin of the same blood, a young woman who, though educated at Cambridge, was careful to display no Western influences in her own country. The wedding day was announced, and the young prince had made a journey to England, bringing with him some of the famous jewels of his house to be reset in appropriate modern settings by Cartier. They had included a very famous ruby, which had been removed from its cumbersome old-fashioned necklace and had been given a new look by the famous jewelers. So far so good, but afterward came the snag. It was not to be supposed that a young man possessed of much wealth and convivial tastes should not commit a few follies of the pleasanter type. As to that there would have been no censure. Young princes were supposed to amuse themselves in this fashion. For the prince to take the girl friend of the moment for a walk down Bond Street and bestow upon her an emerald bracelet or a diamond clip as a reward for the pleasure she had afforded him would have been regarded as quite natural and suitable, corresponding in fact to the Cadillacs that his father invariably presented to his favorite dancing girl of the moment.

But the prince had been far more indiscreet than that. Flattered by the lady's interest, he had displayed to her the famous ruby in its new setting and had finally been so unwise as to accede to her request to be allowed to wear it—just for one evening!

The sequel was short and sad. The lady retired from their supper table to powder her nose. Time passed. She did not return. She had left the establishment by another door and since then had disappeared into space. The important and distressing thing was that the ruby in its new setting had disappeared with her.

These were the facts that could not possibly be made public without the most dire consequences. The ruby was something more than a ruby, it was a historical possession of great significance, and the circumstances of its disappearance were such that any undue publicity about them might result in the most serious political consequences.

Mr. Jesmond was not the man to put these facts into simple language. He wrapped them up, as it were, in a great deal of verbiage. Who exactly Mr. Jesmond was, Hercule Poirot did not exactly know. He had met other Mr. Jesmonds in the course of his career. Whether he was connected with the Home Office, the Foreign Office, or some more discreet branch of public service was not specified. He was acting in the interests of the Commonwealth. The ruby must be recovered.

M. Poirot, so Mr. Jesmond delicately insisted, was the man to recover it.

"Perhaps—yes," Hercule Poirot admitted, "but you can tell me so little. Suggestion—suspicion—all that is not very much to go upon."

"Come now, Monsieur Poirot, surely it is not beyond your powers. Ah, come now."

"I do not always succeed."

But this was mock modesty. It was clear enough from

Poirot's tone that for him to undertake a mission was almost synonymous with succeeding in it.

"His Highness is very young," Mr. Jesmond said. "It will be sad if his whole life is to be blighted for a mere youthful indiscretion."

Poirot looked kindly at the downcast young man. "It is the time for follies, when one is young," he said encouragingly, "and for the ordinary young man it does not matter so much. The good papa, he pays up; the family lawyer, he helps to disentangle the inconvenience; the young man, he learns by experience. All ends for the best. In a position such as yours, it is hard indeed. Your approaching marriage. . . ."

"That is it. That is it exactly." For the first time words poured from the young man. "You see, she is very, very serious. She takes life very seriously. She has acquired at Cambridge many very serious ideas. There is to be education in my country. There are to be schools. There are to be many things. All in the name of progress, you understand, of democracy. It will not be, she says, as it was in my father's time. Naturally she knows that I will have diversions in London, but not the scandal. No! It is the scandal that matters. You see, it is very, very famous, this ruby. There is a long trail behind it, a history. Much bloodshed—many deaths!"

"Deaths," said Hercule Poirot thoughtfully. He looked at Mr. Jesmond. "One hopes," he said, "it will not come to that?"

Mr. Jesmond made a peculiar noise rather like a hen that has decided to lay an egg and then thought better of it.

"No, no, indeed," he said, sounding rather prim. "There is no question, I am sure, of anything of *that* kind."

"You cannot be sure," said Hercule Poirot. "Whoever

has the ruby now, there may be others who want to gain possession of it and who will not stick at a trifle, my friend."

"I really don't think," said Mr. Jesmond, sounding more prim than ever, "that we need enter into speculations of that kind. Quite unprofitable."

"Me," said Hercule Poirot, suddenly becoming very foreign, "me, I explore all the avenues, like the politicians."

Mr. Jesmond looked at him doubtfully. Pulling himself together, he said, "Well, I can take it that is settled, Monsieur Poirot? You will go to Kings Lacey?"

"And how do I explain myself there?" asked Hercule Poirot.

Mr. Jesmond smiled with confidence. "That, I think, can be arranged very easily," he said. "I can assure you that it will all seem quite natural. You will find the Laceys most charming. Delightful people."

"And you do not deceive me about the oil-fired central heating?"

"No, no, indeed." Mr. Jesmond sounded quite pained. "I assure you, you will find every comfort."

"*Tout confort moderne*," murmured Poirot to himself, reminiscently. "*Eh bien*," he said, "I accept."

The temperature in the long drawing room at Kings Lacey was a comfortable sixty-eight as Hercule Poirot sat talking to Mrs. Lacey by one of the big mullioned windows. Mrs. Lacey was engaged in needlework. She was not doing petit point or embroidering flowers upon silk. Instead, she appeared to be engaged in the prosaic task of hemming dishcloths. As she sewed she talked in a soft, reflective voice that Poirot found very charming.

"I hope you will enjoy our Christmas party here, Monsieur Poirot. It's only the family, you know. My granddaughter and a grandson and a friend of his and Bridget, who's my great-niece, and Diana, who's a cousin, and David Welwyn, who is a very old friend. Just a family party. But Edwina Morecombe said that that's what you really wanted to see. An old-fashioned Christmas. Nothing could be more old-fashioned than we are! My husband, you know, absolutely lives in the past. He likes everything to be just as it was when he was a boy of twelve years old and used to come here for his holidays." She smiled to herself. "All the same old things, the Christmas tree and the stockings hung up and the oyster soup and the turkey—two turkeys, one boiled and one roast—and the plum pudding with the ring and the bachelor's button and all the rest of it in it. We can't have sixpences nowadays because they're not pure silver anymore. But all the old desserts, the Elvas plums and Carlsbad plums and almonds and raisins, and crystallized fruit and ginger. Dear me, I sound like a catalogue from Fortnum and Mason!"

"You arouse my gastronomic juices, madame."

"I expect we'll have frightful indigestion by tomorrow evening," said Mrs. Lacey. "One isn't used to eating so much nowadays, is one?"

She was interrupted by some loud shouts and whoops of laughter outside the window. She glanced out. "I don't know what they're doing out there. Playing some game or other, I suppose. I've always been so afraid, you know, that these young people would be bored by our Christmas here. But not at all, it's just the opposite. Now my own son and daughter and their friends, they used to be rather sophisticated about Christmas. Say it was all nonsense and too much fuss and it would be far better to go out to a hotel somewhere and dance. But the younger generation seem to find all this terribly attractive. Besides," added Mrs. Lacey practically, "schoolboys and schoolgirls are always hungry, aren't they? I think they must starve them

177

at these schools. After all, one does know children of that age each eat about as much as three strong men."

Poirot laughed and said, "It is most kind of you and your husband, madame, to include me in this way in your family party."

"Oh, we're both delighted, I'm sure," said Mrs. Lacey. "And if you find Horace a little gruff," she continued, "pay no attention. It's just his manner, you know."

What her husband, Colonel Lacey, had actually said was, "Can't think why you want one of these damned foreigners here cluttering up Christmas. Why can't we have him some other time? Can't stick foreigners! All right, all right, so Edwina Morecombe wished him on us. What's it got to do with *her*, I should like to know? Why doesn't *she* have him for Christmas?"

"Because you know very well," Mrs. Lacey had said, "that Edwina always goes to Claridge's."

Her husband had looked at her piercingly and said, "Not up to something, are you, Em?"

"Up to something?" said Em, opening very blue eyes. "Of course not. Why should I be?"

Old Colonel Lacey laughed, a deep, rumbling laugh. "I wouldn't put it past you, Em," he said. "When you look your most innocent is when you *are* up to something."

Revolving these things in her mind, Mrs. Lacey went on. "Edwina said she thought perhaps you might help us. . . . I'm sure I don't know quite how, but she said that friends of yours had once found you very helpful in—in a case something like ours. I—well, perhaps you don't know what I'm talking about?"

Poirot looked at her encouragingly. Mrs. Lacey was close on seventy, as upright as a ramrod, with snow-white hair, pink cheeks, blue eyes, a ridiculous nose, and a determined chin.

The Theft of the Royal Ruby

"If there is anything I can do, I shall be only too happy to do it," said Poirot. "It is, I understand, a rather unfortunate matter of a young girl's infatuation."

Mrs. Lacey nodded. "Yes. It seems extraordinary that I should—well, want to talk to you about it. After all, you *are* a perfect stranger. . . ."

"*And* a foreigner," said Poirot, in an understanding manner.

"Yes," said Mrs. Lacey, "but perhaps that makes it easier, in a way. Anyhow, Edwina seemed to think that you might perhaps know something—how shall I put it? —something useful about this young Desmond Lee-Wortley."

Poirot paused a moment to admire the ingenuity of Mr. Jesmond and the ease with which he had made use of Lady Morecombe to further his own purposes.

"He has not, I understand, a very good reputation, this young man?" he began delicately.

"No, indeed, he hasn't! A very bad reputation! But that's no help so far as Sarah is concerned. It's never any good, is it, telling young girls that men have a bad reputation? It—it just spurs them on!"

"You are so very right," said Poirot.

"In my young day," went on Mrs. Lacey. "(Oh dear, that's a very long time ago!) We used to be warned, you know, against certain young men, and of course it *did* heighten one's interest in them, and if one could possibly manage to dance with them, or to be alone with them in a dark conservatory. . . ." She laughed. "That's why I wouldn't let Horace do any of the things he wanted to do."

"Tell me," said Poirot, "exactly what is it that troubles you?"

"Our son was killed in the war," said Mrs. Lacey. "My daughter-in-law died when Sarah was born so that she

179

has always been with us, and we've brought her up. Perhaps we've brought her up unwisely—I don't know. But we thought we ought always to leave her as free as possible."

"That is desirable, I think," said Poirot. "One cannot go against the spirit of the times."

"No," said Mrs. Lacey, "that's just what I felt about it. And, of course, girls nowadays do do these sort of things."

Poirot looked at her inquiringly.

"I think the way one expresses it," said Mrs. Lacey, "is that Sarah has got in with what they call the coffee-bar set. She won't go to dances or come out properly or be a deb or anything of that kind. Instead she has two rather unpleasant rooms in Chelsea down by the river, and she wears these funny clothes that they like to wear and black stockings or bright-green ones. Very thick stockings. (So prickly, I always think!) And she goes about without washing or combing her hair."

"*Ça, c'est tout à fait naturelle,*" said Poirot. "It is the fashion of the moment. They grow out of it."

"Yes, I know," said Mrs. Lacey. "I wouldn't worry about *that* sort of thing. But, you see, she's taken up with this Desmond Lee-Wortley, and he really has a *very* unsavory reputation. He lives more or less on well-to-do girls. They seem to go quite mad about him. He very nearly married the Hope girl, but her people got her made a ward in court or something. And of course that's what Horace wants to do. He says he must do it for her protection. But I don't think it's really a good idea, Monsier Poirot. I mean, they'll just run away together and go to Scotland or Ireland or the Argentine or somewhere and either get married or else live together without getting married. And although it may be contempt of court and all that—well, it isn't really an answer, is it, in the end? Especially if a baby's coming. One has to give in then and let them get married. And then, nearly always, it seems to me, after a year or two there's a divorce. The girl comes home, and usually after a year or two she marries someone so nice he's almost dull and settles down. But it's particularly sad, it seems to me, if there is a child, because it's not the same thing, being brought up by a stepfather, however nice. No, I think it's much better if we did as we did in my young days. I mean the first young man one fell in love with was *always* someone undesirable. I remember I had a horrible passion for a young man called—now what was his name?—how strange it is, I can't remember his Christian name at all! Tibbitt, that was his surname. Young Tibbitt. Of course, my father more or less forbade him the house, but he used to get asked to the same dances, and we used to dance together. And sometimes we'd escape and sit out together and occasionally friends would arrange picnics to which we both went. Of course, it was all very exciting and forbidden and one enjoyed it enormously. But one didn't go to the—well, to the *lengths* that girls go nowadays. And so, after a while, the Mr. Tibbitts faded out. And do you know, when I saw him four years later I was surprised what I could *ever* have seen in him! He seemed to be such a *dull* young man. Flashy, you know. No interesting conversation."

"One always thinks the days of one's own youth are best," said Poirot, somewhat sententiously.

"I know," said Mrs. Lacey. "It's tiresome, isn't it? I mustn't be tiresome. But all the same I *don't* want Sarah, who's a dear girl really, to marry Desmond Lee-Wortley. She and David Welwyn, who is staying here, were always such friends and so fond of each other, and we did hope,

Horace and I, that they would grow up and marry. But of course she just finds him dull now, and she's absolutely infatuated with Desmond."

"I do not quite understand, madame," said Poirot. "You have him here now, staying in the house, this Desmond Lee-Wortley?"

"That's *my* doing," said Mrs. Lacey. "Horace was all for forbidding her to see him and all that. Of course, in Horace's day the father or guardian would have called at the young man's lodgings with a horsewhip! Horace was all for forbidding the fellow the house, and forbidding the girl to see him. I told him that was quite the wrong attitude to take. 'No,' I said. 'Ask him down here. We'll have him for Christmas with the family party.' Of course, my husband said I was mad! But I said, 'At any rate, dear, let's *try* it. Let her see him in *our* atmosphere and *our* house and we'll be very nice to him and very polite, and perhaps then he'll seem less interesting to her.'"

"I think, as they say, you *have* something there, madame," said Poirot. "I think your point of view is very wise. Wiser than your husband's."

"Well, I hope it is," said Mrs. Lacey doubtfully. "It doesn't seem to be working much yet. But of course he's been here only a couple of days." A sudden dimple showed in her wrinkled cheek. "I'll confess something to you, Monsieur Poirot. I myself can't help liking him. I don't mean I *really* like him, with my *mind*, but I can feel the charm, all right. Oh, yes, I can see what Sarah sees in him. But I'm an old enough woman and have enough experience to know that he's absolutely no good. Even if I *do* enjoy his company. Though I do think," added Mrs. Lacey, rather wistfully, "he has *some* good points. He asked if he might bring his sister here, you know. She's had an operation and was in the hospital. He said it was so sad for her being in a nursing home over Christmas, and he wondered if it would be too much trouble if he could bring her with him. He said he'd take all her meals up to her and all that. Well now, I do think that *was* rather nice of him, don't you, Monsieur Poirot?"

"It shows a consideration," said Poirot thoughtfully, "which seems almost out of character."

"Oh, I don't know. You can have family affections at the same time as wishing to prey on a rich young girl. Sarah will be *very* rich, you know, not only with what we leave her—and of course that won't be very much because most of the money goes with the place to Colin, my grandson. But her mother was a very rich woman, and Sarah will inherit all her money when she's twenty-one. She's only twenty now. No, I do think it was nice of Desmond to mind about his sister. And he didn't pretend she was anything very wonderful or that. She's a shorthand typist, I gather—does secretarial work in London. And he's been as good as his word and does carry up trays to her. Not all the time, of course, but quite often. So I think he has some nice points. But all the same," said Mrs. Lacey with great decision, "I don't want Sarah to marry him."

"From all I have heard and been told," said Poirot, "that would indeed be a disaster."

"Do you think it would be possible for you to help us in any way?" asked Mrs. Lacey.

"I think it is possible, yes," said Hercule Poirot, "but I do not wish to promise too much. For the Mr. Desmond Lee-Wortleys of this world are clever, madame. But do not despair. One can, perhaps, do a little something. I shall at any rate put forth my best endeavors, if only in gratitude for your kindness in asking me here for this Christmas festivity." He looked around him. "And it cannot be so easy these days to have Christmas festivities."

"No, indeed." Mrs. Lacey sighed. She leaned forward. "Do you know, Monsieur Poirot, what I really dream of —what I would love to have?"

"But tell me, madame."

"I simply long to have a small, modern bungalow. No, perhaps not a bungalow exactly, but a small, modern, easy-to-run house built somewhere in the park here, with an absolutely up-to-date kitchen and no long passages. Everything easy and simple."

"It is a very practical idea, madame."

"It's not practical for me," said Mrs. Lacey. "My husband *adores* this place. He *loves* living here. He doesn't mind being slightly uncomfortable, he doesn't mind the inconveniences, and he would hate, simply *hate*, to live in a small modern house in the park!"

"So you sacrifice yourself to his wishes?"

Mrs. Lacey drew herself up. "I do not consider it a sacrifice, Monsieur Poirot," she said. "I married my husband with the wish to make him happy. He has been a good husband to me and made me very happy all these years, and I wish to give happiness to him."

"So you will continue to live here," said Poirot.

"It's not really too uncomfortable," said Mrs. Lacey.

"No, no," said Poirot hastily. "On the contrary, it is most comfortable. Your central heating and your bath water are perfection."

"We spent a lot of money in making the house comfortable to live in," said Mrs. Lacey. "We were able to sell some land. Ripe for development, I think they call it. Fortunately out of sight of the house on the other side of the park. Really rather an ugly bit of ground with no nice view, but we got a very good price for it. So that we have been able to have as many improvements as possible."

"But the service, madame?"

"Oh, well, that presents less difficulty than you might think. Of course, one cannot expect to be looked after and waited upon as one used to be. Different people come in from the village. Two women in the morning, another two to cook lunch and wash it up, and different ones again in the evening. There are plenty of people who want to come and work for a few hours a day. Of course, for Christmas we were very lucky. My dear Mrs. Ross always comes in every Christmas. She is a wonderful cook, really first class. She retired about ten years ago, but she comes in to help us in any emergency. Then there is dear Peverell."

"Your butler?"

"Yes. He is pensioned off and lives in the little house near the lodge, but he is so devoted, and he insists on coming to wait on us at Christmas. Really, I'm terrified, Monsieur Poirot, because he's so old and so shaky that I feel certain that if he carries anything heavy he will drop it. It's really an agony to watch him. And his heart is not good, and I'm afraid of his doing too much. But it would hurt his feelings dreadfully if I did not let him come. He hems and hahs and makes disapproving noises when he sees the state our silver is in, and within three days of being here, it is all wonderful again. Yes. He is a dear faithful friend." She smiled at Poirot. "So you see, we are all set for a happy Christmas. A white Christmas, too," she added, as she looked out the window. "See? It is beginning to snow. Ah, the children are coming in. You must meet them, Monsieur Poirot."

Poirot was introduced with due ceremony. First, to Colin and Michael, the schoolboy grandson and his friend, nice polite lads of fifteen, one dark, one fair. Then to their cousin Bridget, a black-haired girl of about the same age with enormous vitality.

"And this is my granddaughter, Sarah," said Mrs. Lacey.

Agatha Christie

Poirot looked with some interest at Sarah, an attractive
girl with a mop of red hair; her manner seemed to him
nervy and a trifle defiant, but she showed real affection
for her grandmother.

"And this is Mr. Lee-Wortley."

Mr. Lee-Wortley wore a fisherman's jersey and tight
black jeans; his hair was rather long, and it seemed doubt-
ful whether he had shaved that morning. In contrast to
him was a young man introduced as David Welwyn, who
was solid and quiet, with a pleasant smile, and rather
obviously addicted to soap and water. There was one other
member of the party, a handsome, rather intense-looking
girl who was introducted as Diana Middleton.

Tea was brought in: a hearty meal of scones, crumpets,
sandwiches, and three kinds of cake. The younger members
of the party appreciated the tea. Colonel Lacey came in
last, remarking in a noncommittal voice, "Hey, tea? Oh
yes, tea."

He received his cup of tea from his wife's hand, helped
himself to two scones, cast a look of aversion at Desmond
Lee-Wortley, and sat down as far away from him as he
could. He was a big man with bushy eyebrows and a red,
weather-beaten face. He might have been taken for a
farmer rather than the lord of the manor. "Started to
snow," he said. "It's going to be a white Christmas all
right."

After tea the party dispersed.

"I expect they'll go and play with their tape recorders
now," said Mrs. Lacey to Poirot. She looked indulgently
after her grandson as he left the room. Her tone was that
of one who says, "The children are going to play with their
toy soldiers."

"They're frightfully technical, of course," she said, "and
very grand about it all."

The boys and Bridget, however, decided to go along to the lake and see if the ice on it was likely to make skating possible.

"I thought we could have skated on it this morning," said Colin. "But old Hodgkins said no. He's always so terribly careful."

"Come for a walk, David," said Diana Middleton softly. David hesitated for half a moment, his eyes on Sarah's red head. She was standing by Desmond Lee-Wortley, her hand on his arm, looking up into his face.

"All right," said David Welwyn, "yes, let's."

Diana slipped a quick hand through his arm, and they turned toward the door into the garden.

Sarah said, "Shall we go, too, Desmond? It's fearfully stuffy in the house."

"Who wants to walk?" said Desmond. "I'll get my car out. We'll go along to the Speckled Boar and have a drink."

Sarah hesitated for a moment before saying, "Let's go to Market Ledbury to the White Hart. It's much more fun."

Though for all the world she would not have put it into words, Sarah had an instinctive revulsion from going down to the local pub with Desmond. It was somehow not in the tradition of Kings Lacey. The women of Kings Lacey had never frequented the bar of the Speckled Boar. She had an obscure feeling that to go there would be to let old Colonel Lacey and his wife down. And why not? Desmond Lee-Wortley would have said. For an exasperated moment Sarah felt that he ought to know why not! One didn't upset such old darlings as Grandfather and dear old Em unless it was necessary. They'd been very sweet, really, letting her lead her own life, not understanding in the least why she wanted to live in Chelsea in the way she did, but accepting it. That was due to Em, of course. Grandfather would have kicked up no end of a row.

Sarah had no illusions about her grandfather's attitude. It was not his doing that Desmond had been asked to stay at Kings Lacey. That was Em; Em was a darling and always had been.

When Desmond had gone to fetch his car, Sarah popped her head into the drawing room again.

"We're going over to Market Ledbury," she said. "We thought we'd have a drink there at the White Hart."

There was a slight amount of defiance in her voice, but Mrs. Lacey did not seem to notice it.

"Well, dear," she said, "I'm sure that will be very nice. David and Diana have gone for a walk, I see. I'm so glad. I really think it was a brainwave on my part to ask Diana here. So sad being left a widow so young—only twenty-two—I do hope she marries again *soon*."

Sarah looked at her sharply. "What are you up to, Em?"

"It's my little plan," said Mrs. Lacey gleefully. "I think she's just right for David. Of course I know he was terribly in love with *you*, Sarah dear, but you'd no use for him, and I realize that he isn't your type. But I don't want him to go on being unhappy, and I think Diana will really suit him."

"What a matchmaker you are, Em," said Sarah.

"I know," said Mrs. Lacey. "Old women always are. Diana's quite keen on him already, I think. Don't you think she'd be just right for him?"

"I shouldn't say so," said Sarah. "I think Diana's far too—well, too intense, too serious. I should think David would find it terribly boring being married to her."

"Well, we'll see," said Mrs. Lacey. "Anyway, *you* don't want him, do you dear?"

"No, indeed," said Sarah very quickly. She added in a sudden rush, "You *do* like Desmond, don't you, Em?"

"I'm sure he's very nice indeed," said Mrs. Lacey.

"Grandfather doesn't like him," said Sarah.

"Well, you could hardly expect him to, could you?" said Mrs. Lacey reasonably. "But I dare say he'll come around when he gets used to the idea. You mustn't rush him, Sarah dear. Old people are very slow to change their minds, and your grandfather *is* rather obstinate."

"I don't care what Grandfather thinks or says," said Sarah. "I shall get married to Desmond whenever I like!"

"I know, dear, I know. But do try and be realistic about it. Your grandfather could cause a lot of trouble, you know. You're not of age yet. In another year you can do as you please. I expect Horace will have come around long before that."

"You're on my side, aren't you, darling?" said Sarah. She flung her arms around her grandmother's neck and gave her an affectionate kiss.

"I want you to be happy," said Mrs. Lacey. "Ah! There's your young man bringing his car around. You know, I like these very tight trousers the young men wear nowadays. They look so smart—only, of course, it does accentuate knock-knees."

Yes, Sarah thought, Desmond *has* got knock-knees. She had never noticed it before. . . .

"Go on, dear, enjoy yourself," said Mrs. Lacey.

She watched her go out to the car, then, remembering her foreign guest, she went along to the library. Looking in, however, she saw that Hercule Poirot was taking a pleasant little nap, and, smiling to herself, she went across the hall and out into the kitchen to have a conference with Mrs. Ross.

* * *

"Come on, beautiful," said Desmond. "Your family cutting up rough because you're coming out to a pub? Years behind the times here, aren't they?"

"Of course they're not making a fuss," said Sarah sharply, as she got into the car.

"What's the idea of having that foreign fellow down? He's a detective, isn't he? What needs detecting here?"

"Oh, he's not here professionally," said Sarah. "Edwina Morecombe, my godmother, asked us to have him. I think he's retired from professional work long ago."

"Sounds like a broken-down old cab horse," said Desmond.

"He wanted to see an old-fashioned English Christmas, I believe," said Sarah vaguely.

Desmond laughed scornfully. "Such a lot of tripe, that sort of thing," he said. "How you can stand it, I don't know."

Sarah's red hair was tossed back, and her aggressive chin shot up. "I enjoy it!" she said defiantly.

"You can't, baby. Let's cut the whole thing tomorrow. Go over to Scarborough or somewhere."

"I couldn't possibly do that."

"Why not?"

"Oh, it would hurt their feelings."

"Oh, bilge! You know you don't enjoy this childish, sentimental bosh."

"Well, not really perhaps, but. . . ." Sarah broke off. She realized with a feeling of guilt that she was looking forward a good deal to the Christmas celebration. She enjoyed the whole thing, but she was ashamed to admit that to Desmond. It was not the thing to enjoy Christmas and family life. Just for a moment she wished that Desmond had not come down at Christmas time. In fact, she almost wished that Desmond had not come down at all. It was much more fun seeing him in London than here at home.

In the meantime, the boys and Bridget were walking back from the lake, still discussing earnestly the problems of skating. Flecks of snow had been falling, and looking up at the sky it could be prophesied that before long there was going to be a heavy snowfall.

"It's going to snow all night," said Colin. "Bet you by Christmas morning we have a couple of feet of snow."

The prospect was a pleasurable one.

"Let's make a snowman," said Michael.

"Good lord," said Colin, "I haven't made a snowman since—well, since I was about four years old."

"I don't believe it's a bit easy to do," said Bridget. "I mean, you have to know how."

"We might make an effigy of Monsieur Poirot," said Colin. "Give it a big black mustache. There is one in the dressing-up box."

"I don't see, you know," said Michael thoughtfully, "how Monsieur Poirot could ever have been a detective. I don't see how he'd ever be able to disguise himself."

"I know," said Bridget, "and one can't imagine him running about with a microscope and looking for clues or measuring footprints."

"I've got an idea," said Colin. "Let's put on a show for him!"

"What do you mean, a show?" asked Bridget.

"Well, arrange a murder for him."

"What a gorgeous idea," said Bridget. "Do you mean a body in the snow—that sort of thing?"

"Yes. It would make him feel at home, wouldn't it?"

Bridget giggled. "I don't know that I'd go as far as that."

"If it snows," said Colin, "we'll have the perfect setting.

191

A body and footprints—we'll have to think that out rather carefully and pinch one of Grandfather's daggers and make some blood."

They came to a halt and, oblivious to the rapidly falling snow, entered into an excited discussion.

"There's a paintbox in the old schoolroom. We could mix up some blood—crimson lake, I should think."

"Crimson lake's a bit too pink, *I* think," said Bridget. "It ought to be a bit browner."

"Who's going to be the body?" asked Michael.

"I'll be the body," said Bridget quickly.

"Oh, look here," said Colin, "*I* thought of it."

"Oh, no, no," said Bridget, "it must be me. It's got to be a girl. It's more exciting. Beautiful girl lying lifeless in the snow."

"Beautiful girl! Ah-ha," said Michael in derision.

"I've got black hair, too," said Bridget.

"What's that got to do with it?"

"Well, it'll show up well on the snow, and I shall wear my red pajamas."

"If you wear red pajamas, they won't show the bloodstains," said Michael in a practical manner.

"But they'd look so effective against the snow," said Bridget, "and they've got white facings, you know, so the blood could be on them. Oh, won't it be gorgeous? Do you think he will really be taken in?"

"He will if we do it well enough," said Michael. "We'll have just your footprints in the snow and one other person's going to the body and coming away from it—a man's, of course. He won't want to disturb them, so he won't know that you're not really dead. You don't think—" Michael stopped, struck by a sudden idea. The others looked at him. "You don't think he'll be *annoyed* about it?"

"Oh, I shouldn't think so," said Bridget, with facile optimism. "I'm sure he'll understand that we've done it to entertain him. A sort of Christmas treat."

"I don't think we ought to do it on Christmas Day," said Colin reflectively. "I don't think Grandfather would like that very much."

"Boxing Day then," said Bridget.

"Boxing Day would be just right," said Michael.

"And it'll give us more time, too," pursued Bridget. "After all, there are a lot of things to arrange. Let's go and have a look at the props."

They hurried into the house.

The evening was a busy one. Holly and mistletoe had been brought in in large quantities and a Christmas tree had been set up at one end of the dining room. Everyone helped to decorate it, to put up the branches of holly behind pictures, and to hang mistletoe in a convenient position in the hall.

"I had no idea anything so archaic still went on," murmured Desmond to Sarah with a sneer.

"We've always done it," said Sarah defensively.

"What a reason!"

"Oh, don't be tiresome, Desmond. *I* think it's fun."

"Sarah, my sweet, you *can't!*"

"Well, not—not really, perhaps, but—I do in a way."

"Who's going to brave the snow and go to midnight mass?" asked Mrs. Lacey at twenty minutes to twelve.

"Not me," said Desmond. "Come on, Sarah."

With a hand on her arm he guided her into the library and went over to the record case.

"There are limits, darling," said Desmond. "Midnight mass!"

"Yes," said Sarah. "Oh, yes."

With a good deal of laughter, donning of coats, and stamping of feet, most of the others got off. The two boys, Bridget, David, and Diana set out for the ten minutes' walk to the church through the falling snow. Their laughter died away in the distance.

"Midnight mass!" said Colonel Lacey, snorting. "Never went to midnight mass in my young days. *Mass,* indeed! Popish, that is! Oh, I beg your pardon, Monsieur Poirot."

Poirot waved a hand. "It is quite all right. Do not mind me."

"Matins is good enough for anybody, I should say," said the colonel. "Proper Sunday morning service. 'Hark the Herald Angels Sing,' and all the good old Christmas hymns. And then back to Christmas dinner. That's right, isn't it, Em?"

"Yes, dear," said Mrs. Lacey. "That's what *we* do. But the young ones enjoy the midnight service. And it's nice, really, that they *want* to go."

"Sarah and that fellow don't want to go."

"Well, there dear, I think you're wrong," said Mrs. Lacey. "Sarah, you know, *did* want to go, but she didn't like to say so."

"Beats me why she cares what that fellow's opinion is."

"She's very young really," said Mrs. Lacey placidly. "Are you going to bed, Monsieur Poirot? Good night. I hope you'll sleep well."

"And you, madame? Are you not going to bed yet?"

"Not just yet," said Mrs. Lacey. "I've got the stockings to fill, you see. Oh, I know they're all practically grown up, but they do *like* their stockings. One puts jokes in them! Silly little things. But it all makes for a lot of fun."

"You work very hard to make this a happy house at Christmastime," said Poirot. "I honor you." He raised her hand to his lips in a courtly fashion.

"Hm," grunted Colonel Lacey, as Poirot departed. "Flowery sort of fellow. Still—he appreciates you."

Mrs. Lacey dimpled up at him. "Have you noticed, Horace, that I'm standing under the mistletoe?" she asked with the demureness of a girl of nineteen.

Hercule Poirot entered his bedroom. It was a large room well provided with radiators. As he went over toward the big four-poster bed he noticed an envelope lying on his pillow. He opened it and drew out a piece of paper. On it was a shakily printed message in capital letters.

DON'T EAT NONE OF THE PLUM PUDDING. ONE AS WISHES YOU WELL.

Hercule Poirot stared at it. His eyebrows rose. "Cryptic," he murmured, "and most unexpected."

Christmas dinner took place at two o'clock and was a feast indeed. Enormous logs crackled merrily in the wide fireplace, and above their crackling rose the babel of many tongues talking together. Oyster soup had been consumed, two enormous turkeys had come and gone, mere carcasses of their former selves. Now, the supreme moment, the Christmas pudding was brought in, in state! Old Peverell, his hands and his knees shaking with the weakness of eighty years, permitted no one but himself to bear it in. Mrs. Lacey sat, her hands pressed together in nervous apprehension. One Christmas, she felt sure, Peverell would fall down dead. Having either to take the risk of letting him fall down dead or of hurting his feelings to such an extent that he would probably prefer to be dead than alive, she had so far chosen the former alternative. On a silver dish the Christmas pudding reposed in its glory. A large football of a pudding, a piece of holly stuck in it like a triumphant flag and glorious flames of blue and red rising around it. There was a cheer and cries of "Ooh-ah."

One thing Mrs. Lacey had done: prevailed upon Peverell to place the pudding in front of her so that she could serve it rather than hand it in turn around the table. She breathed a sigh of relief as it was deposited safely in front of her. Rapidly the plates were passed around, flames still licking the portions.

"Wish, Monsieur Poirot," cried Bridget. "Wish before the flame goes. Quick, Gran darling, quick."

Mrs. Lacey leaned back with a sigh of satisfaction. Operation Pudding had been a success. In front of everyone was a helping with flames still licking it. There was a momentary silence all around the table as everyone wished hard.

There was nobody to notice the rather curious expression on the face of Monsieur Poirot as he surveyed the portion of pudding on his plate. "Don't eat none of the plum pudding." What on earth did that sinister warning mean? There could be nothing different about his portion of plum pudding from that of everyone else! Sighing as he admitted himself baffled—and Hercule Poirot never liked to admit himself baffled—he picked up his spoon and fork.

"Hard sauce, Monsieur Poirot?"

Poirot helped himself appreciatively to hard sauce.

"Swiped my best brandy again, eh Em?" said the colonel good-humoredly from the other end of the table.

Mrs. Lacey twinkled at him. "Mrs. Ross insists on having the best brandy, dear," she said. "She says it makes all the difference."

"Well, well," said Colonel Lacey, "Christmas comes but once a year, and Mrs. Ross is a great woman. A great woman and a great cook."

"She is indeed," said Colin. "Smashing plum pudding, this. Mmmmm." He filled an appreciative mouth.

Gently, almost gingerly, Hercule Poirot attacked his portion of pudding. He ate a mouthful. It was delicious! He ate another. Something tinkled faintly on his plate. He investigated with a fork. Bridget, on his left, came to his aid.

"You've got something, Monsieur Poirot," she said. "I wonder what it is."

Poirot detached a little silver object from the surrounding raisins that clung to it.

"Oooh," said Bridget, "it's the bachelor's button! Monsieur Poirot's got the bachelor's button!"

Hercule Poirot dipped the small silver button into the finger bowl of water that stood by his plate and washed it clear of pudding crumbs. "It is very pretty," he observed.

"That means you're going to be a bachelor, Monsieur Poirot," explained Colin helpfully.

"That is to be expected," said Poirot gravely. "I have been a bachelor for many long years, and it is unlikely that I shall change that status now."

"Oh, never say die," said Michael. "I saw in the paper that someone of ninety-five married a girl of twenty-two the other day."

"You encourage me," said Hercule Poirot.

Colonel Lacey uttered a sudden exclamation. His face became purple, and his hand went to his mouth.

"Confound it, Emmeline," he roared, "why on earth do you let the cook put glass in the pudding?"

"Glass!" cried Mrs. Lacey, astonished.

Colonel Lacey withdrew the offending substance from his mouth. "Might have broken a tooth," he grumbled. "Or swallowed the damn thing and had appendicitis."

He dropped the piece of glass into the finger bowl, rinsed it, and held it up. "God bless my soul," he ejaculated. "It's a red stone out of one of the cracker brooches." He held it aloft.

"You permit?" Very deftly Monsieur Poirot stretched across his neighbor, took it from Colonel Lacey's fingers, and examined it attentively. As the squire had said, it was an enormous red stone the color of a ruby. The light gleamed from its facets as he turned it about. Somewhere around the table a chair was pushed sharply back and then drawn in again.

"Phew!" cried Michael. "How wizard it would be if it was *real*."

"Perhaps it *is* real," said Bridget hopefully.

"Oh, don't be an ass, Bridget. Why a ruby of that size would be worth thousands and thousands and thousands of pounds. Wouldn't it, Monsieur Poirot?"

"It would indeed," said Poirot.

"But what *I* can't understand," said Mrs. Lacey, "is how it got into the pudding."

"Oooh," said Colin, diverted by his last mouthful, "I've got the pig. It isn't fair."

Bridget chanted immediately, "Colin's got the pig! Colin's got the pig! Colin is the greedy guzzling *pig!*"

"I've got the ring," said Diana in a clear, high voice.

"Good for you, Diana. You'll be married first of us all."

"I've got the thimble," wailed Bridget.

"Bridget's going to be an old maid," chanted the two boys. "Yah, Bridget's going to be an old maid."

"Who's got the money?" demanded David. "There's a

real ten-shilling piece, gold, in this pudding. I know. Mrs. Ross told me so."

"I think I'm the lucky one," said Desmond Lee-Wortley.

Colonel Lacey's two next-door neighbors heard him mutter, "Yes, you would be."

"*I've* got a ring, too," said David. He looked across at Diana. "Quite a coincidence, isn't it?"

The laughter went on. Nobody noticed that Monsieur Poirot carelessly, as though thinking of something else, had dropped the red stone into his pocket.

Mince pies and Christmas dessert followed the pudding. The older members of the party then retired for a welcome siesta before the tea-time ceremony of the lighting of the Christmas tree. Hercule Poirot, however, did not take a siesta. Instead, he made his way to the enormous old-fashioned kitchen.

"It is permitted," he asked, looking around and beaming, "that I congratulate the cook on this marvelous meal that I have just eaten?"

There was a moment's pause, and then Mrs. Ross came forward in a stately manner to greet him. She was a large woman, nobly built, with all the dignity of a stage duchess. Two lean gray-haired women were beyond in the scullery washing up, and a tow-haired girl, was moving to and fro between the scullery and the kitchen. But they were obviously mere myrmidons. Mrs. Ross was the queen of the kitchen quarters.

"I am glad to hear you enjoyed it, sir," she said graciously.

"Enjoyed it!" cried Hercule Poirot. With an extravagant foreign gesture he raised his hand to his lips, kissed it, and wafted the kiss to the ceiling. "But you are a genius,

Mrs. Ross! A genius! *Never* have I tasted such a wonderful meal. The oyster soup"—he made an expressive noise with his lips—"and the stuffing. The chestnut stuffing in the turkey, that was quite unique in my experience."

"Well, it's funny that you should say that, sir," said Mrs. Ross graciously. "It's a very special recipe, that stuffing. It was given me by an Austrian chef that I worked with many years ago. But all the rest," she added, "is just good, plain English cooking."

"And is there anything better?" demanded Hercule Poirot.

"Well, it's nice of you to say so, sir. Of course, you being a foreign gentleman might have preferred the continental style. Not but what I can't manage continental dishes, too."

"I am sure, Mrs. Ross, you could manage anything! But you must know that English cooking—*good* English cooking, not the cooking one gets in the second-class hotels or the restaurants—is much appreciated by gourmets on the continent, and I believe I am correct in saying that a special expedition was made to London in the early eighteen hundreds, and a report sent back to France of the wonders of the English puddings. 'We have nothing like that in France,' they wrote. 'It is worth making a journey to London just to taste the varieties and excellencies of the English puddings.' And above all puddings," continued Poirot, well launched now on a kind of rhapsody, "is the Christmas plum pudding, such as we have eaten today. That was a homemade pudding, was it not? Not a bought one?"

"Yes, indeed, sir. Of my own making and my own recipe such as I've made for many, many years. When I came here, Mrs. Lacey said that she'd ordered a pudding from a London store to save me the trouble. But no, madame, I said, that may be kind of you, but no bought pudding from a store can equal a homemade Christmas one. Mind you," said Mrs. Ross, warming to her subject like the artist she was, "it was made too soon before the day. A good Christmas pudding should be made some weeks before and allowed to wait. The longer they're kept, within reason, the better they are. I mind now that when I was a child and we went to church every Sunday, we'd start listening for the collect that begins 'Stir up O Lord we beseech thee' because that collect was the signal, as it were, that the puddings should be made that week. And so they always were. We had the collect on the Sunday, and that week sure enough my mother would make the Christmas puddings. And so it should have been here this year. As it was, that pudding was made only three days ago, the day before you arrived, sir. However, I kept to the old custom. Everyone in the house had to come out into the kitchen and have a stir and make a wish. That's an old custom, sir, and I've always held to it."

"Most interesting," said Hercule Poirot. "Most interesting. And so everyone came out into the kitchen?"

"Yes, sir. The young gentlemen, Miss Bridget, the London gentleman who's staying here, and his sister and Mr. David and Miss Diana—Mrs. Middleton, I should say. . . . All had a stir, they did."

"How many puddings did you make? Is this the only one?"

"No, sir, I made four. Two large ones and two smaller ones. The other large one I planned to serve on New Year's Day, and the smaller ones were for Colonel and Mrs. Lacey when they're alone like and not so many in the family."

201

"I see, I see," said Poirot.

"As a matter of fact, sir," said Mrs. Ross, "it was the wrong pudding you had for lunch today."

"The wrong pudding?" Poirot frowned. "How is that?"

"Well, sir, we have a big Christmas mold. A china mold with a pattern of holly and mistletoe on top, and we always have the Christmas Day pudding boiled in that. But there was a most unfortunate accident. This morning, when Annie was getting it down from the shelf in the larder, she slipped and dropped it and it broke. Well, sir, naturally I couldn't serve that, could I? There might have been splinters in it. So we had to use the other one—the New Year's Day one, which is in a plain bowl. It's nice, but it's not so decorative as the Christmas mold. Really, where we'll get another mold like that I don't know. They don't make things in that size nowadays. All tiddly bits of things. Why, you can't even buy a breakfast dish that'll take a proper eight to ten eggs and bacon. Ah, things aren't what they were."

"No, indeed," said Poirot. "But today that is not so. This Christmas Day has been like the Christmas Days of old, is that not true?"

Mrs. Ross sighed. "Well, I'm glad you say so, sir, but of course I haven't the *help* now that I used to have. Not skilled help, that is. The girls nowadays"—she lowered her voice slightly—"they mean very well and they're very willing, but they've not been *trained,* sir, if you understand what I mean."

"Times change, yes," said Hercule Poirot. "I, too, find it sad sometimes."

"This house, sir," said Mrs. Ross. "It's too large, you know, for the mistress and the colonel. The mistress, she knows that. Living in a corner of it as they do, it's not the same thing at all. It only comes alive, as you might say, at Christmastime when all the family gather."

"It is the first time, I think that Mr. Lee-Wortley and his sister have been here?"

"Yes, sir." A note of slight reserve crept into Mrs. Ross's voice. "A very nice gentleman he is, but. . . . Well, it seems a funny friend for Miss Sarah to have, according to our ideas. But there—London ways are different! It's sad that his sister's so poorly. Had an operation, she had. She seemed all right the first day she was here, but that very day, after we'd been stirring the puddings, she was took bad again, and she's been in bed ever since. Got up too soon after her operation, I expect. Ah, doctors nowadays, they have you out of the hospital before you can hardly stand on your feet. Why, my very own nephew's wife. . . ." And Mrs. Ross went into a long and spirited tale of hospital treatment as accorded to her relations, comparing it unfavorably with the consideration that had been lavished upon them in older times.

Poirot duly commiserated with her. "It remains," he said, "to thank you for this exquisite and sumptuous meal. You permit a little acknowledgment of my appreciation?" A crisp five-pound note passed from his hand into that of Mrs. Ross, who said perfunctorily, "You really shouldn't do *that*, sir."

"I insist. I insist."

"Well, it's very kind of you indeed, sir." Mrs. Ross accepted the tribute as no more than her due. "And I wish you, sir, a very happy Christmas and a prosperous New Year."

The end of Christmas Day was like the end of most Christmas Days. The tree was lighted, a splendid Christmas cake came in for tea, was greeted with approval but was partaken of only moderately. There was cold supper.

Both Poirot and his host and hostess went to bed early.

"Good night, Monsieur Poirot," said Mrs. Lacey. "I hope you've enjoyed yourself."

"It has been a wonderful day, madame, wonderful."

"You're looking very thoughtful," said Mrs. Lacey.

"It is the English pudding that I consider."

"You found it a little heavy perhaps?" asked Mrs. Lacey delicately.

"No, no, I do not speak gastronomically. I consider its significance."

"It's traditional, of course," said Mrs. Lacey. "Well, good night, Monsieur Poirot, and don't dream too much of Christmas puddings and mince pies."

"Yes," murmured Poirot to himself, as he undressed. "It is a problem certainly, that Christmas plum pudding. There is here something that I do not understand at all." He shook his head in a vexed manner. "Well, we shall see."

After making certain preparations, Poirot went to bed, but not to sleep.

It was some two hours later that his patience was rewarded. The door of his bedroom opened very gently. He smiled to himself. It was as he had thought it would be. His mind went back fleetingly to the cup of coffee so politely handed him by Desmond Lee-Wortley. A little later, when Desmond's back was turned, he had laid the cup down for a few moments on a table. He had then apparently picked it up again, and Desmond had had the satisfaction, if satisfaction it was, of seeing him drink the coffee to the last drop. But a little smile lifted Poirot's mustache as he reflected that it was not he but someone else who was sleeping a good sound sleep tonight. "That pleasant young David," said Poirot to himself, "he is worried, unhappy. It will do him no harm to have a night's really sound sleep. And now let us see what will happen."

He lay quite still, breathing in an even manner with occasionally a suggestion, but the very faintest suggestion, of a snore.

Someone came up to the bed and bent over him. Then, satisfied, that someone turned away and went to the dressing table. By the light of a tiny torch the visitor was examining Poirot's belongings neatly arranged on top of the dressing table. Fingers explored the wallet, gently pulled open the drawers of the dressing table, then extended the search to the pockets of Poirot's clothes. Finally the visitor approached the bed and with great caution slid his hand under the pillow. Withdrawing his hand, he stood for a moment or two as though uncertain what to do next. He walked around the room looking inside ornaments, went into the adjoining bathroom from whence he presently returned. Then, with a faint exclamation of disgust, he went out of the room.

"Ah," said Poirot, under his breath, "you have a disappointment. Yes, yes, a serious disappointment. Bah! To imagine even that Hercule Poirot would hide something where you could find it!" Then, turning over on his other side, he went peacefully to sleep.

He was aroused next morning by an urgent soft tapping on his door.

"*Qui est là?* Come in, come in."

The door opened. Breathless, red-faced, Colin stood upon the threshold. Behind him stood Michael.

205

"Monsieur Poirot, Monsieur Poirot."

"But yes?" Poirot sat up in bed. "It is the early tea? But no. It is you, Colin. What has occurred?"

Colin was for a moment speechless. He seemed to be under the grip of some strong emotion. In actual fact it was the sight of the nightcap that Hercule Poirot wore that affected for the moment his organs of speech. Presently he controlled himself and spoke. "I think—Monsieur Poirot, could you help us? Something rather awful has happened."

"Something has happened? But what?"

"It's—it's Bridget. She's out there in the snow. I think —she doesn't move or speak and—oh, you'd better come and look for yourself. I'm terribly afraid—she may be dead."

"What?" Poirot cast aside his bedcovers. "Mademoiselle Bridget—dead!"

"I think—I think somebody's killed her. There's—there's blood and—oh do come!"

"But certainly. But certainly. I come on the instant."

With great practicality Poirot inserted his feet into his outdoor shoes and pulled a fur-lined overcoat over his pajamas. "I come," he said. "I come on the moment. You have aroused the house?"

"No. No, so far I haven't told anyone but you. I thought it would be better. Grandfather and Gran aren't up yet. They're laying breakfast downstairs, but I didn't say anything to Peverell. She—Bridget—she's around the other side of the house, near the terrace and the library window."

"I see. Lead the way. I will follow."

Turning away to hide his delighted grin, Colin led the way downstairs. They went out through the side door. It was a clear morning with the sun not yet high over the horizon. It was not snowing now, but it had snowed heavily during the night, and everywhere around was an unbroken carpet of thick snow. The world looked very pure and white and beautiful.

"There!" said Colin breathlessly. "I—it's—*there!*" He pointed dramatically.

The scene was indeed dramatic enough. A few yards away Bridget lay in the snow. She was wearing scarlet pajamas and a white wool wrap thrown around her shoulders. The white wool wrap was stained with crimson. Her head was turned aside and hidden by the mass of her outspread black hair. One arm was under her body, the other lay flung out, the fingers clenched, and standing up in the center of the crimson stain was the hilt of a large curved Kurdish knife that Colonel Lacey had shown to his guests only the evening before.

"*Mon Dieu!*" ejaculated Monsieur Poirot. "It is like something on the stage!"

There was a faint choking noise from Michael.

Colin thrust himself quickly into the breach. "I know," he said. "It—it doesn't seem *real* somehow, does it? Do you see those footprints? I suppose we mustn't disturb them."

"Ah, yes, the footprints. No, we must be careful not to disturb those footprints."

"That's what I thought," said Colin. "That's why I wouldn't let anyone go near her until we got you. I thought you'd know what to do."

"All the same," said Hercule Poirot, "first we must see if she is still alive. Is not that so?"

"Well—yes—of course," said Michael, a little doubtfully, "but you see, we thought—I mean, we didn't like. . . ."

"Ah, you have the prudence! You have read the detective stories. It is most important that nothing should be touched and that the body should be left as it is. But we cannot be sure as yet if it *is* a body, can we? After all,

Agatha Christie

though prudence is admirable, common humanity comes first. We must think of the doctor, must we not, before we think of the police?"

"Oh, yes. Of course," said Colin, still a little taken aback.

"We only thought—I mean—we thought we'd better get you before we did anything," said Michael hastily.

"Then you will both remain here," said Poirot. "I will approach from the other side so as not to disturb these footprints. Such excellent footprints, are they not? So very clear. The footprints of a man and a girl going out together to the place where she lies. And then the man's footsteps come back, but the girl's do not."

"They must be the footprints of the murderer," said Colin with bated breath.

"Exactly," said Poirot. "The footprints of the murderer. A long narrow foot with rather a peculiar type of shoe. Very interesting. Easy, I think, to recognize. Yes, those footprints will be very important."

At that moment Desmond Lee-Wortley came out of the house with Sarah and joined them. "What on earth are you all doing here?" he demanded in a somewhat theatrical manner. "I saw you from my bedroom window. What's up? Good lord, what's this? It—it looks like. . . ."

"Exactly," said Hercule Poirot. "It looks like murder, does it not?"

Sarah gave a gasp, then shot a quick, suspicious glance at the two boys.

"You mean someone's killed the girl—what's-her-name—Bridget?" demanded Desmond. "Who on earth would want to kill her? It's unbelievable!"

"There are many things that are unbelievable," said Poirot. "Especially before breakfast, is it not? That is what one of your classics says. Six impossible things before breakfast." He added, "Please wait here, all of you."

Carefully making a circuit, he approached Bridget and bent down for a moment over the body. Colin and Michael were now both shaking with suppressed laughter.

Sarah joined them, murmuring, "What have you two been up to?"

"Good old Bridget," whispered Colin. "Isn't she wonderful? Not a twitch!"

"I've never seen anything look as dead as Bridget does," whispered Michael.

Hercule Poirot straightened up again. "This is a terrible thing," he said. His voice held an emotion it had not held before.

Overcome by mirth, Michael and Colin both turned away. In a choked voice Michael said, "What—what must we do?"

"There is only one thing to do," said Poirot. "We must send for the police. Will one of you telephone, or would you prefer me to do it?"

"I think," said Colin, "I think— What about it, Michael?"

"Yes," said Michael, "I think the jig's up now." He stepped forward. For the first time he seemed a little unsure of himself. "I'm awfully sorry," he said, "I hope you won't mind too much. It—er—it was a sort of joke for Christmas and all that, you know. We thought we'd— well, lay on a murder for you."

"You thought you would lay on a murder for me? Then this—then this. . . ."

"It's just a show we put on," explained Colin, "to—to make you feel at home, you know."

"Aha," said Hercule Poirot. "I understand. You make of me the April fool, is that it? But today is not April the first, it is December the twenty-sixth."

"I suppose we oughtn't to have done it really," said

Colin, "but—but—you don't mind very much, do you, Monsieur Poirot? Come on, Bridget," he called, "get up. You must be half-frozen to death already."

The figure in the snow, however, did not stir.

"It is odd," said Hercule Poirot. "She does not seem to hear you." He looked thoughtfully at them. "It is a joke, you say? You are sure this is a joke?"

"Why, yes." Colin spoke uncomfortably. "We—we didn't mean any harm."

"But why then does Mademoiselle Bridget not get up?"

"I can't imagine," said Colin.

"Come on, Bridget," said Sarah impatiently. "Don't go on lying there playing the fool."

"We really are very sorry, Monsieur Poirot," said Colin apprehensively. "We do really apologize."

"You need not apologize," said Poirot in a peculiar tone.

"What do you mean?" Colin stared at him. He turned again. "Bridget! Bridget! What's the matter? Why dosen't she get up? Why does she go on lying there?"

Poirot beckoned to Desmond. "*You*, Mr. Lee-Wortley. Come here. . . ."

Desmond joined him.

"Feel her pulse," said Poirot.

Desmond Lee-Wortley bent down. He touched the arm —the wrist.

"There's no pulse. . . ." He stared at Poirot. "Her arm's stiff. Good God she really *is* dead!"

Poirot nodded. "Yes, she is dead," he said. "Someone has turned the comedy into a tragedy."

"Someone—who?"

"There is a set of footprints going and returning. A set of footprints that bears a strong resemblance to the footprints *you* have just made, Mr. Lee-Wortley, coming from the path to this spot."

Desmond Lee-Wortley wheeled around. "What on earth. . . . Are you accusing me? *Me*? You're crazy! Why on earth should I want to kill the girl?"

"Ah—why? I wonder. . . . Let us see. . . ." He bent down and very gently prised open the stiff fingers of the girl's clenched hand.

Desmond drew a sharp breath. He gazed down unbelievingly. In the palm of the dead girl's hand was what appeared to be a large ruby. "It's that damn thing out of the pudding!" he cried.

"Is it?" said Poirot. "Are you sure?"

"Of course it is."

With a swift movement Desmond bent down and plucked the red stone out of Bridget's hand.

"You should not do that," said Poirot reproachfully. "Nothing should have been disturbed."

"I haven't disturbed the body, have I? But this thing might—might get lost, and it's evidence. The important thing is to get the police here as soon as possible. I'll go at once and telephone." He wheeled around and ran sharply toward the house.

Sarah came swiftly to Poirot's side. "I don't understand," she whispered. Her face was dead white. "I don't *understand*." She caught at Poirot's arm. "What did you mean about—about the footprints?"

"Look for yourself, mademoiselle."

The footprints that led to the body and back again were the same as the ones just made accompanying Poirot to the girl's body and back.

"You mean—that it was Desmond? Nonsense!"

Suddenly the noise of a car came through the clear air. They wheeled around. They saw the car clearly enough, driving at a furious pace down the drive, and Sarah recognized what car it was.

211

"It's Desmond," she said. "It's Desmond's car. He—he must have gone to fetch the police instead of telephoning."

Diana Middleton came running out of the house to join them. "What's happened?" she cried in a breathless voice. "Desmond just came rushing into the house. He said something about Bridget being killed, and then rattled the telephone but it was dead. He couldn't get any answer. He said the wires must have been cut. He said the only thing was to take a car and go for the police. Why the police?"

Poirot made a gesture.

"Bridget?" Diana stared at him. "But surely—isn't it a joke of some kind? I heard something—something last night. I thought that they were going to play a joke on you, Monsieur Poirot?"

"Yes," said Poirot, "that was the idea—to play a joke on me. But now come into the house, all of you. We shall catch our deaths of cold here, and there is nothing to be done until Mr. Lee-Wortley returns with the police."

"But look here," said Colin, "we can't—we can't leave Bridget here alone."

"You can do her no good by remaining," said Poirot gently. "Come, it is a sad, a very sad tragedy, but there is nothing we can do anymore to help Mademoiselle Bridget. So let us come in and get warm and have perhaps a cup of tea or of coffee."

They followed him obediently into the house. Peverell was just about to ring the gong. If he thought it extraordinary for most of the household to be outside and for Poirot to make an appearance in pajamas and an overcoat, he displayed no sign of it. Peverell in his old age was still the perfect butler. He noticed nothing that he was not asked to notice. They went into the dining room and sat down.

When they all had a cup of coffee in front of them and were sipping it, Poirot spoke.

"I have to recount to you," he said, "a little history. I cannot tell you all the details, no. But I can give you the main outline. It concerns a young princeling who came to this country. He brought with him a famous jewel, which he was to have reset for the lady he was going to marry, but unfortunately before that he made friends with a very pretty young lady. This pretty young lady did not care very much for the man, but she did care for his jewel —so much so that one day she disappeared with this historic possession that had belonged to his house for generations. So the poor young man, he is in a quandary, you see. Above all he cannot have a scandal. Impossible to go to the police. Therefore he comes to me, Hercule Poirot. 'Recover for me,' he says, 'my historic ruby.' *Eh bien,* this young lady, she has a friend, and the friend, he has put through several very questionable transactions. He has been concerned with blackmail, and he has been concerned with the sale of jewelry abroad. Always he has been very clever. He is suspected, yes, but nothing can be proved. It comes to my knowledge that this very clever gentleman, he is spending Christmas here in this house. It is important that the pretty young lady, once she has acquired the jewel, should disappear for a while from circulation, so that no pressure can be put upon her, no questions can be asked her. It is arranged, therefore, that she comes here to Kings Lacey, ostensibly as the sister of the clever gentleman. . . ."

Sarah drew a sharp breath. "Oh, no. Oh, no, not *here!* Not with me here!"

"But so it is," said Poirot. "And by a little manipulation I, too, become a guest here for Christmas. This young lady, she is supposed to have just come out of the hospital.

She is much better when she arrives here. But then comes the news that I, too, arrive, a detective—a well-known detective. At once she has what you call the wind up. She hides the ruby in the first place she can think of, and then very quickly she has a relapse and takes to her bed again. She does not want that I should see her, for doubtless I have a photograph and shall recognize her. It is very boring for her, yes, but she has to stay in her room, and her brother, he brings up the trays."

"And the ruby?" demanded Michael.

"I think," said Poirot, "that at the moment it is mentioned I arrive, the young lady was in the kitchen with the rest of you, all laughing and talking and stirring the Christmas puddings. The Christmas puddings are put into bowls, and the young lady, she hides the ruby, pressing it down into one of the pudding bowls. Not the one that we are going to have on Christmas Day. Oh, no, that one she knows is in a special mold. She puts it in the other one, the one that is destined to be eaten on New Year's Day. Before then she will be ready to leave, and when she leaves no doubt that Christmas pudding will go with her. But see how fate takes a hand. On the very morning of Christmas Day there is an accident. The Christmas pudding in its fancy mold is dropped on the stone floor, and the mold is shattered to pieces. So what can be done? The good Mrs. Ross, she takes the other pudding and sends it in."

"Good lord," said Colin, "do you mean that on Christmas Day when Grandfather was eating his pudding that was a *real* ruby he'd got in his mouth?"

"Precisely," said Poirot, "and you can imagine the emotions of Mr. Desmond Lee-Wortley when he saw that. *Eh bien,* what happens next? The ruby is passed around. I examine it and manage unobtrusively to slip it in my pocket. In a careless way as though I were not interested. But one person at least observes what I have done. When I lie in bed, that person searches my room. He searches me. He does not find the ruby. Why?"

"Because," said Michael breathlessly, "you had given it to Bridget. That's what you mean. And so that's why—but I don't understand quite—I mean. . . . Look here, what *did* happen?"

Poirot smiled at him. "Come now into the library," he said, "and look out of the window, and I will show you something that may explain the mystery."

He led the way and they followed him.

"Consider once again," said Poirot, "the scene of the crime."

He pointed out the window. A simultaneous gasp broke from the lips of all of them. There was no body lying on the snow, no trace of the tragedy seemed to remain except a mass of scuffled snow.

"It wasn't all a dream, was it?" said Colin faintly. "I—has someone taken the body away?"

"Ah," said Poirot. "You see? The Mystery of the Disappearing Body." He nodded his head, and his eyes twinkled gently.

"Good lord," cried Michael. "Monsieur Poirot, you are—you haven't—oh, look here, he's been having us on all this time!"

Poirot twinkled more than ever. "It is true, my children. I also have had my little joke. I knew about your little plot, you see, and so I arranged a counterplot of my own. Ah, *voilà* Mademoiselle Bridget. None the worse, I hope, for your exposure in the snow? Never should I forgive myself if you caught *une fluxion de poitrine*."

Bridget had just come into the room. She was wearing a thick skirt and a woollen sweater. She was laughing.

Agatha Christie

"I sent a *tisane* to your room," said Poirot severely. "You have drunk it?"

"One sip was enough!" said Bridget. "I'm all right. Did I do it well, Monsieur Poirot? Goodness, my arm hurts still after that tourniquet you made me put on it."

"You were splendid, my child," said Poirot. "Splendid. But see, all the others are still in the fog. Last night I went to Mademoiselle Bridget. I told her that I knew about your little *complot,* and I asked her if she would act a part for me. She did it very cleverly. She made the footprints with a pair of Mr. Lee-Wortley's shoes."

Sarah said in a harsh voice, "But what's the point of it all, Monsieur Poirot? What's the point of sending Desmond off to fetch the police? They'll be very angry when they find out it's nothing but a hoax."

Poirot shook his head gently. "But I do not think for one moment, mademoiselle, that Mr. Lee-Wortley went to fetch the police," he said. "Murder is a thing in which Mr. Lee-Wortley does not want to be mixed up. He lost his nerve badly. All he could see was his chance to get the ruby. He snatched that, he pretended the telephone was out of order, and he rushed off in a car on the pretense of fetching the police. I think myself it is the last you will see of him for some time. He has, I understand, his own ways of getting out of England. He has his own plane, has he not, mademoiselle?"

Sarah nodded. "Yes," she said. "We were thinking of. . . ." She stopped.

"He wanted you to elope with him that way, did he not? *Eh bien,* that is a very good way of smuggling a jewel out of the country. When you are eloping with a girl, and that fact is publicized, then you will not be suspected of also smuggling a historic jewel out of the country. Oh, yes, that would have made a very good camouflage."

216

"I don't believe it," said Sarah. "I don't believe a word of it!"

"Then ask his sister," said Poirot, gently nodding his head over her shoulder. Sarah turned her head sharply.

A platinum blonde stood in the doorway. She wore a fur coat and was scowling. She was clearly in a furious temper. "Sister my foot!" she said, with a short unpleasant laugh. "That swine's no brother of mine! So he's beaten it, has he, and left me to carry the can? The whole thing was *his* idea! *He* put me up to it! Said it was money for jam. They'd never prosecute because of the scandal. I could always threaten to say that Ali had *given* me his historic jewel. Des and I were to have shared the swag in Paris—and now the swine runs out on me! I'd like to murder him!" She switched abruptly. "The sooner I get out of here. . . . Can someone telephone for a taxi?"

"A car is waiting at the front door to take you to the station, mademoiselle," said Poirot.

"Think of everything, don't you?"

"Most things," said Poirot complacently.

But Poirot was not to get off so easily. When he returned to the dining room after assisting the spurious Miss Lee-Wortley into the waiting car, Colin was waiting for him.

There was a frown on his boyish face. "But look here, Monsieur Poirot. What about the ruby? Do you mean to say you've let him get away with it?"

Poirot's face fell. He twirled his mustaches. He seemed ill at ease. "I shall recover it yet," he said weakly. "There are other ways. I shall still. . . ."

"Well, I do think!" said Michael. "To let that swine get away with the ruby!"

Bridget was sharper. "He's having us on again," she cried. "You are, aren't you, Monsieur Poirot?"

Agatha Christie

"Shall we do a final conjuring trick, mademoiselle? Feel in my left-hand pocket."

Bridget thrust her hand in. She drew it out again with a scream of triumph and held aloft a large ruby blinking in crimson splendor.

"You comprehend," exclaimed Poirot, "the one that was clasped in your hand was a paste replica. I brought it from London in case it was possible to make a substitution. You understand? We do not want the scandal. Monsieur Desmond will try and dispose of that ruby in Paris or in Belgium or wherever it is that he has his contacts, and then it will be discovered that the stone is not real! What could be more excellent? All finishes happily. The scandal is avoided, my princeling receives his ruby back again, he returns to his country and makes a sober and we hope a happy marriage. All ends well."

"Except for me," murmured Sarah under her breath.

She spoke so low that no one heard her but Poirot. He shook his head gently. "You are in error, Mademoiselle Sarah, in what you say there. You have gained experience. All experience is valuable. Ahead of you I prophesy there lies happiness."

"That's what *you* say," said Sarah.

"But look here, Monsieur Poirot." Colin was frowning. "How did you know about the show we were going to put on for you?"

"It is my business to know things," said Hercule Poirot. He twirled his mustache.

"Yes, but I don't see how you could have managed it. Did someone split—did someone come and tell you?"

"No, no, not that."

"Then how? Tell us how?"

They all chorused, "Yes, tell us how."

218

"But no," Poirot protested. "But no. If I tell you how I deduced that, you will think nothing of it. It is like the conjuror who shows how his tricks are done!"

"Tell us, Monsieur Poirot! Go on. Tell us, tell us!"

"You really wish that I should solve for you this last mystery?"

"Yes, go on. Tell us."

"Ah, I do not think I can. You will be so disappointed."

"Now come on, Monsieur Poirot, tell us. How did you know?"

"Well, you see, I was sitting in the library by the window in a chair after tea the other day and reposing myself. I had been asleep, and when I awoke you were discussing your plans just outside the window close to me, and the window was open at the top."

"Is that all?" cried Colin, disgusted. "How simple!"

"Is it not?" cried Hercule Poirot, smiling. "You see? You *are* disappointed!"

"Oh, well," said Michael, "at any rate we know everything now."

"Do we?" murmured Hercule Poirot to himself. "*I* do not. I, whose business it is to know things."

He walked out into the hall, shaking his head a little. For perhaps the twentieth time he drew from his pocket a rather dirty piece of paper.

**DON'T EAT NONE OF THE PLUM PUDDING.
ONE AS WISHES YOU WELL.**

Hercule Poirot shook his head reflectively. He who could explain everything could not explain this! Humiliating. Who had written it? *Why* had it been written? Until he found that out he would never know a moment's

peace. Suddenly he came out of his reverie to be aware
of a peculiar gasping noise. He looked sharply down. On
the floor, busy with a dustpan and brush, was a tow-
headed creature in a flowered overall. She was staring
at the paper in his hand with large, round eyes.

"Oh, sir," said this apparition. "Oh, *sir. Please,* sir."

"And who may you be, *mon enfant?*" inquired Poirot
genially.

"Annie Bates, sir, please sir. I come here to help Mrs.
Ross. I didn't mean, sir, I didn't mean to—to do anything
what I shouldn't do. I did mean it well, sir. For your good,
I mean."

Enlightenment came to Poirot. He held out the dirty
piece of paper. "Did you write that, Annie?"

"I didn't mean any harm, sir. Really I didn't."

"Of course you didn't, Annie." He smiled at her. "But
tell me about it. Why did you write this?"

"Well, it was them two, sir. Mr. Lee-Wortley and his
sister. Not that she *was* his sister, I'm sure. None of us
thought so! And she wasn't ill a bit. We could all tell *that.*
We thought—we all thought—something queer was going
on. I'll tell you straight, sir. I was in her bathroom taking
in the clean towels, and I listened at the door. *He* was in
her room, and they were talking together. I heard what
they said plain as plain. 'This detective,' he was saying.
'This fellow Poirot who's coming here. We've got to do
something about it. We've got to get him out of the way
as soon as possible.' And then he says to her in a nasty,
sinister sort of way, lowering his voice, 'Where did you
put it?' And she answered him, 'In the pudding.' Oh,
sir, my heart gave such a leap I thought it would stop
beating. I thought they meant to poison you in the Christmas pudding. I didn't know *what* to do! Mrs. Ross, she
wouldn't listen to the likes of me. Then the idea came to

me as I'd write you a warning. And I did, and I put it on your pillow where you'd find it when you went to bed." Annie paused breathlessly.

Poirot surveyed her gravely for some minutes. "You see too many sensational films, I think, Annie," he said at last, "or perhaps it is the television that affects you? But the important thing is that you have the good heart and a certain amount of ingenuity. When I return to London I will send you a present."

"Oh, thank you sir. Thank you very much, sir."

"What would you like, Annie, as a present?"

"Anything I like, sir? Could I have anything I like?"

"Within reason," said Hercule Poirot prudently, "yes."

"Oh, sir, could I have a vanity box? A real posh slap-up vanity box like the one Mr. Lee-Wortley's sister wot wasn't his sister had?"

"Yes," said Poirot, "yes, I think that could be managed. It is interesting," he mused. "I was in a museum the other day, observing some antiquities from Babylon or one of those places, thousands of years old, and among them were cosmetics boxes. The heart of woman does not change."

"Beg your pardon, sir?" said Annie.

"It is nothing," said Poirot. "I reflect. You shall have your vanity box, child."

"Oh, thank you, sir. Oh, thank you very much indeed."

Annie departed ecstatically. Poirot looked after her, nodding his head in satisfaction. "Ah," he said to himself. "And now—I go. There is nothing more to be done here."

A pair of arms slipped around his shoulders unexpectedly. "If you *will* stand just under the mistletoe. . . ." said Bridget.

Hercule Poirot enjoyed it. He enjoyed it very much. He said to himself that he had had a very good Christmas.

Phyllis R. Fenner was born in Almond, New York, and for thirty-two years was the librarian of the Plandome Road School in Manhasset, New York. In 1955 she retired and made her permanent home in Manchester, Vermont. She holds degrees from Mount Holyoke College and from the Columbia Library School, and she has traveled extensively throughout this country, Canada, Mexico and Europe.

Miss Fenner's work has brought her in touch with library schools throughout the country; she has also done book reviewing, given lectures about children's books, and held story hours for children. In addition, she is widely known for her many distinguished anthologies.